I0609441

Whistling Sinatra

A Psychological Thriller

Connie Myres

Feather and Fermion Publishing

Copyright © 2025 by Connie Myres
All rights reserved.

Whistling Sinatra

No part of this publication may be reproduced, distributed, or transmitted
in any form or by any means, including photocopying, recording, or other
electronic or mechanical methods, without the prior written permission of
the publisher, except as permitted by U.S. copyright law.

The story, all names, characters, and incidents portrayed in this production
are fictitious. No identification with actual persons (living or deceased),
places, buildings, and products is intended or should be inferred.

Feather and Fermion Publishing
Connie S. Myres
Michigan, USA
ConnieMyres.com

ISBN: 978-1-957819-31-0 (eBook)
ISBN: 978-1-957819-32-7 (hardcover)
ISBN: 978-1-957819-33-4 (paperback)

DEDICATION

To my family and friends—
especially my sons, Lucas and Charles Kraus,
and to Lydia Kraus, Charles' wife—
thank you for your loyal support and constant
encouragement of all my projects.
I appreciate you more than words can say.

1

SATURDAY, JULY 8

Clara dumped her purse onto the kitchen counter for the third time. Wallet, receipts, lip balm, her own keys; everything except what she was looking for.

"They have to be somewhere," Julian said from the doorway. His voice carried that tone she'd been noticing more often lately—patient on the surface, but with frustration underneath.

They'd only been married three months, but she was already learning to read the subtleties.

"I haven't touched your keys." Clara leaned against the counter, trying to steady herself.

Dr. Kaminski had taught her this grounding technique two years ago. *Notice five things you can see. Four you can hear.*

"I know, honey. But they were right there on the hook when we got home last night." Julian moved into the kitchen. "Did you maybe grab them by mistake when you were carrying in the groceries?"

"I used my own keys. I always use my own keys."

"Just check your purse one more time. Check the zippered pockets."

Clara reached into the bag again. She unzipped a pocket she rarely used and found the keys at the bottom. She pulled them out. Julian's BMW key fob.

"Oh."

"See? Mystery solved." Julian took the keys from her, kissing her forehead. "You probably grabbed them without thinking. We all do things like that when we're distracted."

"I don't remember putting them there."

"Memory's a funny thing, Clara. Remember last week when you were sure you'd sent that email to your editor, but it was still in your drafts?" His tone was gentle. "You've been stressed about your deadline. It's completely normal."

Clara nodded, though nothing about this felt normal. She *had* been stressed about her novel deadline. Maybe she was more scattered than she realized. She'd worked so hard with Dr. Kaminski to get her anxiety under control before the wedding. She couldn't be slipping backward already.

Julian's phone rang. He glanced at the screen.

"I need to take this." He was already moving toward his office down the hall. "Work thing."

Clara remained at the counter, staring at the contents of her purse spread across the granite. Through the walls, she could hear Julian's voice. She moved closer to the hallway, catching fragments:

". . . told you not to call this number . . ."

". . . I hear you. August first . . ."

". . . I'll have the funds . . ."

The conversation ended abruptly. Julian emerged from his office, running a hand through his dark hair, a gesture she'd learned meant he was agitated.

"Everything okay?" Clara asked.

"Just a compliance issue. Audit stuff. Very boring, very urgent. You know how these financial regulations can be."

Before Clara could respond, his phone rang again. This time when he looked at the screen, his shoulders relaxed slightly.

"David Morrison," he said. "I swear this man thinks weekends don't exist." He answered with his professional voice: "Julian Thorne speaking."

Clara listened as Julian's side of the conversation grew increasingly concerned. "Slow down, David. What do you mean the entire portfolio?" A pause. "No, don't do anything rash. I can be there in an hour."

He ended the call and looked at Clara apologetically. "I'm so sorry, honey. Morrison's having some kind of crisis about his investments. He's threatening to liquidate everything if I don't come talk him down."

"On a Saturday? We were going to the farmers market."

"I know, I know." Julian was already grabbing his laptop bag. "But Morrison's my biggest client. If he pulls his money, it could seriously damage my reputation. You know how skittish investors can be, one person panics, and suddenly everyone's questioning your judgment."

Clara wanted to protest, but they'd just bought this house near Saugatuck, their first real place as newlyweds. They needed his income.

"How long will you be?"

"Few hours at most. Morrison lives out past Allegan, so there's the drive time." Julian paused in his packing to cup her face in his hands. "You look tired, sweetheart. Why don't you use the quiet time to work on your novel? Or maybe just rest? You've been pushing yourself pretty hard."

"I'm fine."

"Are you?" His thumb stroked her cheek. "Because you seem a little scattered lately. The keys, the missed email to your editor, forgetting about supper with my colleague last week—"

"I didn't forget supper. You never told me about it."

"Clara." His voice was so patient, so concerned. "We talked about it three times. You even wrote it in your planner."

Had she? Clara couldn't remember, which frightened her more than his words. She'd check her planner later.

"Maybe you should consider talking to someone," Julian said. "I mentioned Dr. Graves before, she specializes in stress management. Several of my clients swear by her."

"I'll think about it."

"That's all I ask." He kissed her forehead again, grabbed his bag, and headed for the door. "Try to relax. Maybe sit outside for a bit, the fresh air might help."

After his BMW pulled away, Clara stood in the sudden quiet of their house.

She made herself a cup of tea and settled at her laptop. Detective Sullivan's investigation waited on the screen, cursor blinking patiently at the end of a paragraph.

The evidence had been planted, Sullivan was certain now. But knowing something and proving it were different beasts entirely. The truth was usually hidden in the patterns, in the details that seemed insignificant until you saw how they connected.

Clara stared at the words, then typed a new sentence: *The hardest part wasn't finding the evidence. It was trusting himself enough to believe what it meant.*

The irony wasn't lost on her. Here she was, writing about a detective learning to trust his instincts while she questioned her own memory about something as simple as car keys.

A movement outside caught her eye. In the yard next door, an elderly woman in a purple cardigan was setting up what looked like a large birdcage on her back porch. Clara had seen her a few times since they'd moved in but hadn't introduced herself yet.

Maybe Julian was right about the fresh air.

Clara saved her document and walked outside. The July morning was already warm. She made her way through the gap in the hedge that separated their properties.

"Hello there!" The woman said. "You must be the new neighbor. I'm Mavis Potts."

"Clara Thorne." They shook hands. "We recently moved in."

"Oh, I know, dear. Not much happens on this street without me noticing." Mavis laughed at herself. "That sounds terribly nosy, doesn't it? But when you're retired and live alone, neighborhood watching becomes something of a hobby."

A loud squawk drew Clara's attention to the cage. Inside perched a magnificent African Grey parrot, his feathers ranging from charcoal to pearl, with a striking crimson tail.

"This is Stanley," Mavis said proudly. "Stanley, say hello to Clara."

The parrot tilted his head, studying Clara. Then, in a voice so clear it made Clara jump: "Hello, beautiful! Welcome to the neighborhood!"

"Oh my goodness, that's incredible!"

"He's a character, aren't you, Stanley?" Mavis opened a container of sunflower seeds. "African Greys are amazing mimics. He picks up everything—voices, phones, doorbells. Last week he had me running to answer the microwave when it wasn't even on."

As if to demonstrate, Stanley produced a perfect imitation of a microwave's beeping timer, followed by the sound of a ringing phone.

"See what I mean?" Mavis settled into a wicker chair, gesturing for Clara to take the other. "Sometimes I think he hears better than I do. Picks up sounds from all over the neighborhood."

"Has he learned anything interesting?"

"Oh, all sorts of things. Dog barks, car alarms, someone's jazz music from three houses down. And lately he's been doing this whistling. Some old tune I don't recognize. Must be coming from somewhere nearby."

"The only trouble with Stanley," Mavis added, "is that he's an escape artist. Figured out how to work his cage latch twice now. I'll look out the window and there he is, perched in the trees between our houses, free as you please. Little Houdini, aren't you?"

Stanley squawked as if in agreement, then demonstrated by deftly working the latch with his beak until it clicked open.

"Stanley, no!" Mavis quickly secured the door again. "See what I mean? I really need to get a better lock."

Stanley suddenly launched into a melody Clara recognized immediately, one of those Sinatra standards Julian sometimes hummed while shaving.

"That's—" Clara stopped herself. "That's funny. My husband sometimes whistles old songs."

"Well, mystery solved then! Stanley must have heard him through the windows. These houses are closer than they look, and sound carries something fierce in summer when everyone has their windows open."

They chatted for another few minutes about the neighborhood, the best local restaurants, the peculiarities of the garbage collection schedule. Stanley occasionally interjected with random sounds—a door slam, a cat's meow, someone saying "Where are my glasses?"

"That last one's me," Mavis admitted with a laugh. "I must say it twenty times a day."

Clara was about to excuse herself when Stanley made a new sound, the distinctive purr of an expensive car engine, followed by a man's voice: "It has to look like an accident."

Clara froze. "What did he just say?"

"Oh, who knows? He picks up fragments of conversations, phone calls, TV shows. Half the time I can't tell where he learned what." Mavis shook her head fondly. "Yesterday he kept saying 'batteries not included' over and over. Probably from some commercial."

Clara forced herself to relax. Of course. The parrot could have heard that phrase from any number of sources—a TV crime show, a movie, someone's phone conversation about insurance claims.

"I should probably get back to work," Clara said, standing. "It was lovely meeting you both."

"Anytime, dear. Stanley and I don't get many visitors. It's nice to have young people in the neighborhood again."

As Clara walked back to her house, she heard Stanley behind her, cycling through his repertoire of sounds. A dog barking, a doorbell, then that whistled melody again.

Inside, she checked her planner, running her finger down the past week's entries. There it was: *Supper with Mitchell Reeves, 7 PM, Copper Rock.* But she had no memory of writing it, no memory of Julian telling her about it.

Clara stared at the entry, trying to force the memory to surface. Nothing.

She returned to her laptop, but Detective Sullivan's investigation felt less compelling now. Instead, she pulled out her journal and began writing:

Saturday, July 8th

Something's wrong, but I can't name it. Found J's keys in my purse—impossible. I didn't put them there. But they were there, so I must have. Right?

J got two calls. First one made him tense, something about August 1st and funds. Second was David Morrison, client crisis. Had to leave for emergency meeting.

Memory issues getting worse. Didn't remember supper with Mitchell. But it was in my planner.

Met neighbor Mavis and her parrot. Bird repeats everything he hears. Including something about making something look like an accident. Probably from TV.

J suggests Dr. Graves for stress. Maybe he's right. Maybe I do need help.

Or maybe—

Clara stopped writing, pen hovering over the page. Or maybe what? That her new husband was somehow making her feel crazy? That was ridiculous. Paranoid. Exactly the kind of thinking that had sent her to Dr. Kaminski in the first place.

She closed the journal and returned to her novel. Detective Sullivan needed her attention more than her own unfounded anxieties.

Two hours later, she'd managed to write three solid pages when her phone buzzed with a text from Julian:

Morrison situation worse than expected. Might be a few more hours. Don't wait for lunch. Love you.

Clara looked at the clock, already past noon. Through the window, she could see Mavis's porch was empty now, though she could hear Stanley inside the house, practicing his sounds.

She made herself a sandwich and ate it standing at the kitchen counter, staring at the hook where Julian's keys should have been this morning. Such a small thing. Such a nothing thing.

So why couldn't she shake the feeling that it was the beginning of something larger?

Outside, Stanley let out another burst of sounds—a phone ringing, a door closing, and then that whispered phrase again: "It has to look like an accident."

This time, Clara noticed the voice saying those words sounded familiar. It sounded like Julian.

But that was impossible. Julian was miles away with David Morrison. And besides, the parrot could have learned that phrase weeks ago, from anyone, from anything.

Clara closed the window and returned to her laptop. Detective Sullivan had evidence to analyze, patterns to find, a case to solve. Fiction was so much simpler than reality. In fiction, the clues always led somewhere. In reality, sometimes keys just ended up in the wrong place, and memory played tricks, and parrots repeated random phrases that meant nothing at all.

She began typing:

Sullivan knew he was being paranoid. But in his experience, the difference between paranoia and intuition was usually just a matter of time.

Clara paused, reading the sentence back. Then she saved her document, closed her laptop, and went to double-check that all the doors were locked.

Just in case.

2

SUNDAY, JULY 9TH

CLARA WOKE TO AN empty bed. Julian's side was cold, the sheets barely disturbed, as if he'd slept on top of the covers. The bedside clock read 8:17 AM—later than she usually woke, but her head felt clouded.

She could hear him downstairs, humming something cheerful in the kitchen. The smell of eggs and hollandaise sauce drifted up. Eggs benedict on a Sunday morning, elaborate even for Julian.

His clothes from yesterday lay in a heap by the hamper. As Clara picked them up, she smelled sweat and something like cleaning solution. She moved his dress shoes, finding dried mud caked in the treads. Odd for a client meeting in an office building.

"Morning, beautiful!" Julian called from the bottom of the stairs. "Breakfast is ready when you are."

Clara made her way downstairs, still feeling foggy. Julian stood at the stove, looking refreshed and perfectly put together in khakis and a crisp white shirt. Two plates of eggs benedict waited on the breakfast bar, along with fresh fruit and her coffee cup already filled.

"You didn't have to do all this," Clara said, settling onto a barstool.

"I wanted to. You seemed so restless last night. Tossing and turning." He set orange juice in front of her. "Bad dreams?"

Clara didn't remember any dreams. She didn't remember being restless either. "I don't think so."

"Well, drink your coffee while it's hot. It's that new blend I picked up, supposed to be healthier. Adaptogens or something." He gestured to an expensive-looking bag on the counter. "For stress relief."

Clara took a sip and immediately noticed the taste—bitter. "It's . . . different."

"You'll get used to it. It's good for you." Julian sipped from his own cup without any reaction. "I saw you made good progress on your novel yesterday. That scene with Detective Sullivan in the warehouse was brilliant."

Clara set down her coffee. "How do you know about that scene?"

"You showed me last night, remember? After supper. You were so excited about the breakthrough. You read me the whole chapter."

She had no memory of this. None at all. The last thing she remembered from yesterday was writing at her laptop in the afternoon, then . . . nothing. A complete blank.

"Right," Clara said slowly, taking another sip of the bitter coffee. "Of course."

"Are you feeling okay? You look a little sick."

"I'm fine. Just tired, I guess."

"Well, eat something. You barely touched supper last night."

Clara didn't remember supper either, but she picked up her fork and took a bite of eggs benedict. It was perfectly made. The hollandaise rich and lemony, the English muffin toasted just right. Julian was watching her.

"I should call Aunt Margaret," Clara said, suddenly remembering. "It's Sunday. We always talk on Sunday mornings."

"That's nice that you two stay so connected." Julian scrolled through his tablet.

At 10 AM exactly, Clara dialed Margaret's number. It rang four times, five, six, then went to voicemail. Clara frowned and tried again. Same result.

"That's strange. She always answers on Sunday mornings."

"Maybe she's in the greenhouse," Julian said, not looking up from his tablet. "You know how she gets with those orchids."

Clara sent a text: *Morning Aunt M! Missed our call. Everything okay?*

She set the phone aside and took another sip of coffee. The drowsiness was already creeping in, despite having just woken up. Must be the heavy breakfast.

Five minutes later, her phone buzzed.

Sorry dear! In the greenhouse, dirty hands. How are you?

Clara smiled, relieved. "She's fine. Just in the greenhouse."

"Good,"

They texted back and forth for several minutes. Margaret mentioned her orchids were blooming beautifully, that she'd been organizing papers all week.

Planning to update my will this week. Want to make sure you're properly taken care of.

Clara typed back: *Please don't talk like that. You're going to outlive us all.*

You're the only family I have left who matters. And these stairs are getting creakier every day. Really must get them fixed before someone takes a tumble!

Be careful on those stairs! Love you.

Love you too, dear. Talk next Sunday?

Of course. Every Sunday, always.

Clara set the phone down. Something about the texts felt off. Margaret usually used more exclamation points, more garden-specific details. But then again, maybe she was just busy.

"Everything good with Margaret?" Julian asked casually.

"Yes, she's fine. Just puttering with her plants."

Clara stood to clear the dishes, but the room tilted slightly. She gripped the counter.

"Whoa there." Julian was beside her instantly. "You okay?"

"Just a little dizzy. I think I need to move around."

"I think you need to sit down."

"It's gone now. I must've gotten up too fast."

She headed to the laundry room. As she sorted clothes, she checked Julian's jacket pockets—a habit from her mother, who always said men left everything in their pockets.

She found a small plastic bag. Inside were about a dozen white, round pills with no markings.

"Julian?" She walked back to the kitchen, holding the bag. "What are these?"

He looked up from his tablet, squinting at the bag. For a moment, his face was completely blank. Then he laughed.

"Oh! Those are my supplements. You know, for gut health." He stood and opened a cabinet, pulling out a bottle. "See? I put some in a baggie for the office. Easier than carrying the whole bottle."

He shook one out onto his palm—white, round, identical to the ones in the bag. Clara felt foolish.

"Sorry, I just—"

"Hey." He cupped her face gently. "You're really stressed, aren't you? First the keys yesterday, now this. Maybe you should consider talking to someone. That Dr. Graves I mentioned, several of my clients see her. She specializes in women's mental health."

"I'm fine."

"You seem more anxious than usual."

Clara pulled away. "I said I'm fine. I just need some air."

Outside, the morning was already warm. Mavis was on her porch with Stanley, who was chattering away in his cage.

"Clara! How nice to see you, dear. Stanley's been particularly vocal this morning."

Stanley squawked and then said clearly: "August first. August first."

"That's new," Clara said.

"Oh, he's been at it all morning. Listen to this—" Mavis leaned toward the cage. "Come on, Stanley, show Clara what else you learned."

The parrot tilted his head, then in a man's voice: "Half a million dollars. She won't suspect anything."

Mavis laughed. "Must be picking up phone conversations from somewhere. These houses are so close together."

Then, in a different voice, a woman's voice: "Increase the dosage if needed."

"Is that from a TV show?" Clara asked.

"Who knows? Yesterday evening he was making the strangest sounds, like digging. Rhythmic, you know? Like someone with a shovel." Mavis shook her head. "Oh! And then he said the funniest thing—"

Stanley interrupted with perfect clarity: "It has to look like an accident."

"Too much crime TV in this neighborhood, I think. Someone must be binge-watching those detective shows."

"Must be," Clara said.

Back inside, Julian was washing dishes, something he rarely did without being asked.

"Feeling better?" he asked.

"A little. Julian, did we go for a walk yesterday evening?"

"Of course we did. Down to the lake, remember? You said it would help with your plot problem." He dried his hands and pulled out his phone. "Here, look."

He showed her a photo, the two of them by the lake, sunset golden behind them. Clara was smiling, but her eyes looked wrong. Glassy. Unfocused.

"I don't remember this."

"Honey, you were pretty tired. You'd been writing all day." He swiped to another photo, just the sunset. "You took this one. Said the colors were perfect for a scene you were working on."

Clara checked her own phone. There it was, in her camera roll. 7:43 PM yesterday. But she had no memory of taking it. No memory of the walk. No memory of anything after about 4 PM.

"Maybe I should lie down," she said.

"Good idea. Oh, I spoke to Ted Morrison this morning, David's brother. He said David's doing much better after our talk yesterday. Crisis averted."

Clara nodded absently and headed upstairs. She pulled out her journal from its hiding spot behind other books and wrote quickly:

Sunday, July 9th

Coffee tastes wrong—bitter, medicinal. J says it's new blend.

Can't remember last night at all. Complete blank after 4 PM.

J says we walked to lake. Have photos but no memory.

Found pills in J's pocket—says supplements. They look like regular pills.

Margaret only texted, didn't call. Seemed off somehow.

Stanley repeating concerning things—August 1st, five hundred thousand dollars,

> *"increase the dosage"—woman's voice.*
> *Feel drowsy after coffee. Not normal.*

She photographed the page with her phone, then wrote on a scrap of paper: *Sunday, July 9th—If you don't remember writing this, document everything.* She tucked it under the earrings in her jewelry box.

The rest of the day passed in a fog. Clara tried to write but couldn't focus. She dozed on the couch, waking to find Julian watching her.

"You were out for two hours," he said. "This isn't normal, Clara."

"I know."

"I'm worried about you." He sat beside her, pulling a business card from his wallet. "Dr. Alana Graves. She comes highly recommended. Just think about it?"

Clara took the card. *Dr. Alana Graves, MD. Psychiatry. Specializing in Women's Mental Health.*

"I had lunch with Tom Bradley last week; you remember Tom from the Christmas party? His wife was having similar issues. Anxiety, memory problems, fatigue. Dr. Graves helped her tremendously."

"I'll think about it."

That evening, Julian made supper—grilled salmon, Clara's favorite. She picked at it, still feeling queasy. Around 10 PM, Julian stepped onto the porch to take a call. Clara crept to the window to listen.

"It's done. No complications." His voice was low. "The texts worked perfectly. She didn't suspect anything."

A pause, then: "Increase it tomorrow. We need more documented episodes."

Another pause. "By August first, everything will be in place."

Clara pulled back from the window. Increase what? What episodes? What was happening August first?

Julian came back inside, all smiles. "Sorry about that. Work never really stops, does it?" He turned down the bedding. "You look exhausted, honey. Let's get you to bed."

He disappeared into the bathroom and returned with a glass of water and two white pills. "For your headache."

"I don't have a headache."

"You keep rubbing your temples. Come on, it's just Tylenol."

The pills looked exactly like the ones from the plastic bag. Exactly like the ones in the bottle he'd shown her. Clara took them, placing them on her tongue, taking a sip of water. But as Julian turned away, she tucked them under her tongue, only pretending to swallow.

"Good girl," he said, kissing her forehead. "Let's get some sleep."

In bed, Julian's arm draped over her, his breathing steady. The pills were starting to dissolve under her tongue. When she was sure he was asleep, she turned her head and spit them quietly into a tissue, tucking it under her side of the mattress.

Whatever Julian was giving her, it wasn't Tylenol. And whatever was happening on August first, he and that woman on the phone, the one Stanley had mimicked, were planning something.

Clara lay awake in the dark, Julian's arm heavy across her waist, and tried to remember everything she could about yesterday. But after 4 PM, there was nothing. Just a black hole where her memory should be.

Through the open window, she could hear Stanley in his cage next door, practicing his newest sounds. The woman's voice: "Increase the dosage if needed."

Then Julian's voice: "She won't suspect anything."

Clara closed her eyes and pretended to sleep, while beside her, her husband of three months breathed steadily, his arm tightening around her whenever she moved, as if even in sleep, he was making sure she couldn't get away

3

MONDAY, JULY 10TH

Clara woke alone again. She found the tissue under the mattress; the pills from last night had dissolved into a gritty paste that confirmed what she already knew. Whatever Julian was giving her, it wasn't Tylenol.

Downstairs, Julian hummed in the kitchen. Coffee was already made. Of course it was.

She dressed slowly, steadying herself for another day of pretending to drink that bitter coffee, pretending to swallow whatever pills he offered. Her phone buzzed on the nightstand. Unknown number, but local area code.

"Hello?"

"Ms. Hayes?" The voice was professionally flat. "This is Gideon Krell from Krell & Dimond, LLP. I'm calling regarding your aunt, Margaret Denham."

"Oh, is this about updating her will? She mentioned—"

"Ms. Hayes." A pause. "I'm afraid I have difficult news. Your aunt passed away Saturday evening."

The room tilted. Clara gripped the edge of the nightstand.

"That's not possible. We texted yesterday. Sunday morning. She was in her greenhouse."

"I'm afraid there must be some confusion. Margaret was found at the bottom of her staircase Sunday morning by her housekeeper, Mrs. Lee. The coroner estimates death occurred around Saturday night."

"No. No, we texted. I have the messages—"

"Ms. Hayes, I understand this is shocking. Perhaps you should sit down. Is there someone there with you?"

Julian appeared in the doorway. He crossed the room, taking the phone from her trembling hand.

"This is Julian Thorne, Clara's husband . . . Yes. I see . . . Of course. What arrangements need to be made?"

His free hand settled on her back. A tissue box placed in front of her before she realized she was crying. Julian handled everything, asking about the funeral home, the estate, the necessary paperwork. All the right questions in the right order.

Clara watched him through her tears. He wasn't surprised.

"Yes, we can meet Tuesday morning. Ten o'clock works perfectly." He ended the call and set the phone aside. "Oh, honey. I'm so sorry."

He pulled her against his chest, and she let him.

"How?" Clara pulled back. "She texted me yesterday."

"No, sweetheart. You're confused. The shock; it's completely normal." His thumb wiped tears from her cheek. "She died Saturday night. Fell down those stairs she was always complaining about."

Clara grabbed her phone, scrolling to the messages. There they were—Sunday, 10:05 AM. *Sorry dear! In the greenhouse, dirty hands.*

"Look." She showed him the screen.

Julian studied it. "Honey, check the date again."

She looked. The messages were there, but now they showed Saturday's date. That couldn't be right.

"But I remember—"

"Memory plays tricks during trauma. It's completely normal." He guided her to sit on the bed. "The lawyer said the estate is substantial. Two-point-eight million, plus the house."

"What?"

"Margaret left everything to you. She must have loved you very much." His hand rubbed circles on her back. "That's . . . that's life-changing money, Clara. But don't worry about any of that now. I'll handle everything."

"I should go to the house," Clara said. "See where it happened."

"Not today. You're in shock. You need to process this first." He produced another one of Dr. Graves's business cards from his pocket like a magic trick. "I really think you should talk to someone. She specializes in grief and trauma."

"Julian—"

"Yesterday's memory issues, now this shock. Honey, I'm worried about you. Let me take care of you. Please."

His phone rang.

"I need to take this. Work." He stepped into the hallway. Through the door, Clara caught fragments: "Yes, I heard . . . The timeline is unchanged . . . August first . . ."

Clara rose on unsteady legs and made her way downstairs. The bitter, healthy coffee waited in her favorite cup. She carried it outside, needing air, needing space from Julian's hovering concern.

Mavis stood on her porch, repositioning Stanley's cage to catch the morning sun. Her face crumpled when she saw Clara.

"Oh, dear. I heard about Margaret. Mrs. Lee called me; we're in the same book club. Such a terrible accident."

"Mrs. Lee found her?"

"Sunday morning, yes. The poor woman is beside herself. She said Margaret called her Friday night, worried about strange noises around the house. Margaret thought maybe someone was trying to break in." Mavis shook her head. "At our age, we worry about such things. Living alone in that big house."

Stanley squawked and tilted his head at Clara. Then, in a man's voice: "She never saw me coming."

Clara's coffee cup almost slipped from her hand.

Stanley continued, switching to a woman's voice: "And the wife?"

Man's voice: "Out cold. Your dosage worked perfectly."

The woman: "The stairs?"

The man: "Just like we planned."

A pause, then the woman's voice: "Half a million will solve your problem."

The man: "Two-point-eight, actually."

The woman: "After the funeral. Nothing before."

Then the man: "August first. Everything cleared by August first."

"Oh!" Mavis frowned at the cage. "Stanley, stop that nonsense. He must have picked up some murder mystery from someone's TV, again. The timing is just dreadful, isn't it?"

Clara forced herself to nod. "When did he start saying these things?"

"Just yesterday evening. He was particularly chatty after his little escape adventure Saturday afternoon. Got out again and was gone for hours. Found him in the trees between our houses Sunday morning, happy as could be."

Saturday afternoon, Julian was with David Morrison. When Margaret was still alive. "I should go," Clara said.

Back inside, Julian was off the phone, making lists at the kitchen table. "Feeling better? You look pale."

"I need to check something." Clara pulled up her call log, scrolling to Saturday. No calls to Margaret. Nothing Sunday either, despite the texts.

"What are you looking for?"

"I called Margaret Sunday morning. We always talk Sunday mornings."

"Honey." That patient tone again. "She died Saturday night. You couldn't have called her Sunday."

"But the texts—"

"Clara, you're scaring me." He stood, moving toward her. "This confusion, the memory gaps, it's more than just stress."

He picked up his phone and dialed. "Dr. Graves? It's Julian Thorne. Yes, about my wife. Is that cancellation Wednesday still available? It's become rather urgent."

Clara wanted to protest, but what could she say? That she thought her husband had something to do with Margaret's death? That a parrot was providing evidence? She'd sound insane.

That evening, after funeral arrangements, phone calls with lawyers, sympathetic neighbors stopping by, Julian brought her two white pills and a glass of water.

"For the shock," he said. "Please, Clara. I can't stand seeing you in pain."

"I don't want—"

"Don't you trust me? I'm just trying to help. This is what Dr. Kaminski would want; for you to take care of yourself during trauma."

Clara took the pills, placed them on her tongue, and accepted the water. But she'd been practicing. The pills tucked into the pocket between her gum and cheek as she swallowed the water.

"Thank you," she said, handing him the glass.

"Let me hear you say something else. I want to make sure you're okay."

"I'm just tired, Julian. It's been a horrible day."

He studied her for a long moment, then kissed her forehead. "Get some rest."

Later, after Julian had taken a shower, Clara spat the pills into a tissue and hid them with the others. She retrieved her journal from an old shoebox in the closet; her previous hiding spot behind the books had been disturbed, pages slightly out of order.

Monday, July 10th

Margaret is dead. Saturday night—when J was supposedly with Morrison.

Inherited $2.8 million.

Stanley repeated a man's voice that sounded like J's about half a million. Then a woman saying "after the funeral."

The Sunday texts exist but show Saturday now. How?

J pushing Dr. Graves harder. Thursday appointment.

He's watching me take pills more carefully.

Found my first hiding spot. He's looking for something.

She photographed the entry, then added: *The mud on his shoes.*

Clara couldn't sleep. She stood at the bedroom window, watching clouds pass over the moon. Behind her, Julian shifted in his sleep.

Then silence, except for Julian's snoring. Clara's heart broke for an aunt who had tried to warn her about strange noises, who had died alone on her stairs while her niece slept.

Two-point-eight million dollars. More than enough to kill for.

But what if she was wrong? What if the stress of Margaret's death was making her paranoid, connecting dots that didn't exist? Julian had been nothing but supportive today; handling the lawyer, the funeral arrangements, comforting her. The bitter coffee could just be how the new blend tastes. The pills might really be for her own good. Maybe those fragments Stanley repeated really were from some TV show, and her grief-stricken mind was twisting them into something sinister.

Dr. Kaminski had always warned her about catastrophic thinking, about her tendency to spiral. What kind of wife suspects her husband of murder based on a parrot's mimicry? Maybe Julian was right. Maybe she did need help. Maybe Dr. Graves could help her sort out what was real from what her anxious mind was creating.

Clara returned to bed, lying rigid beside her husband, and wondered if the real danger was her own mind turning against her

4

TUESDAY, JULY 11TH

CLARA WOKE WITH A clearer head than she'd had in days. No Julian beside her, but she could hear him downstairs, cabinets opening and closing. Today was the meeting with the lawyer.

She dressed, choosing the charcoal gray pantsuit Julian had bought her for his company dinner last month. The kind of outfit that said she was handling her grief appropriately.

In the kitchen, Julian had laid out papers across the breakfast bar. Death certificate, bank statements, their marriage certificate. He looked up from his tablet when she entered.

"Coffee's ready." He gestured to her cup, already poured. "That new blend you like."

Clara wrapped her hands around the warm ceramic. "Thank you."

"Krell's office is in Grand Rapids." Julian checked his watch. "We should leave in twenty."

"I could drive myself—"

"Don't be ridiculous. You're grieving." He moved behind her, hands settling on her shoulders. "Besides, these legal things can be overwhelming. You'll want support."

His thumbs pressed into the knots at the base of her neck. Clara took another pretend sip of coffee.

"Did you sleep?" he asked. "I heard you get up around three."

She hadn't realized he'd been awake. "Just restless."

"Maybe Dr. Graves can prescribe something. Help you through this period."

"I haven't even met her yet."

"Tomorrow. After the funeral." His hands stilled. "I managed to get you an appointment. Lucky, really, she's usually booked weeks out."

Clara watched him in the microwave's black reflection.

"Drink your coffee before it gets cold."

She lifted the cup again. This time when she brought it to her lips, he was watching. She had to take a real sip. The bitterness coated her tongue. "Still getting used to the taste."

"It grows on you." He returned to his papers. "The health benefits are worth it. Adaptogens, antioxidants. Good for stress."

Twenty minutes later, they were in his BMW. Julian drove with one hand on the wheel, the other resting on her knee. Classical music played softly, not his usual jazz.

"Have you been to Krell's office before?" Clara asked.

"What? No, why would I have?"

"You didn't put the address in the GPS."

"I looked it up earlier." His hand squeezed her knee gently. "You're very observant today."

"Am I not usually?"

"That's not what I meant." He glanced at her, then back to the road. "You just seem more yourself. Less foggy."

Less drugged, Clara thought but didn't say.

The law offices of Krell & Dimond occupied the top floor of a modern building. All glass and sharp angles. The receptionist offered condolences.

"Mr. Krell will be with you shortly. Can I get you anything? Water? Coffee?"

"We're fine," Julian answered before Clara could speak.

They waited in leather chairs. Julian scrolled through his phone, occasionally frowning at the screen. Clara watched the receptionist, who kept glancing at them over her computer monitor.

"Mr. and Mrs. Thorne?"

Gideon Krell stood in the doorway—tall, thin, wearing a suit that looked like it had never known a wrinkle. His handshake was firm.

"My condolences on your loss."

The conference room was all dark walnut and formal. Krell sat across from them, a thick folder aligned perfectly with the edge of the table. Julian pulled out Clara's chair before taking his own, positioning himself slightly closer to Krell.

"Mrs. Denham's estate is straightforward," Krell began. "She updated her will six days before her death."

Clara looked up. "Six days?"

"Yes. July second. She came in personally, quite insistent about the changes."

"What changes?" Julian asked.

Krell's eyes moved to Julian, then back to Clara. "The primary beneficiary. Previously, the estate was to be divided among several charities. The new will leaves everything to you, Mrs. Thorne."

"Everything?"

"The house in Allegan County, its contents, investment accounts totaling approximately two-point-eight million dollars, and a modest checking account for immediate expenses."

Julian whistled low. "That's . . . substantial."

"Mrs. Denham was a careful investor." Krell pulled out a document. "She also left this. Her instructions were quite specific. It was to be given to Mrs. Thorne privately."

He held out a cream-colored envelope. Clara's name was written across it.

Julian reached for it. "I'll—"

"Privately," Krell repeated. He kept the envelope extended toward Clara.

She took it. "Thank you."

"The estate will need to go through probate," Krell continued. "Typically takes three to four weeks for an estate this size."

"That long?" Julian shifted forward in his chair, the leather creaking.

"Standard procedure. Though there is a provision for immediate expenses—funeral costs, estate maintenance. Up to ten thousand can be released within forty-eight hours."

Krell continued, "Speaking of which, the funeral home has suggested next Monday, the seventeenth. It will give time for the arrangements and for family to be notified."

"Monday is fine. We'll need that time," Julian said. "What about liquid accounts? Checking, savings, CDs that transfer outside probate?"

"Those would be accessible immediately upon death certificate filing," Krell said. "Though I don't have specifics on amounts."

"Ballpark?"

"Mrs. Denham was conservative. Kept substantial cash reserves." Krell paused. "Perhaps six figures in liquid assets, but you'd need to contact her banks directly."

"And after probate?"

"Full access to all accounts and properties."

They discussed paperwork, tax implications, the transfer of deeds. Julian asked most of the questions, his knowledge of estate law surprisingly comprehensive. Clara held Margaret's letter, noting the old-fashioned flourish on the capital C of her name.

"I need to use the restroom," she said.

"Down the hall, second door on the right," Krell said.

Julian started to stand. "I'll show you—"

"I can find it."

In the bathroom, Clara locked the door and leaned against it. She opened the envelope, trying not to tear it.

My dearest Clara,

If you're reading this, then my concerns were justified. I've left you everything not out of sentiment (though I do love you dearly) but because you're the only one who never asked, never expected, never calculated what I was worth.

Someone has been asking questions. A man called three times claiming to be from various utilities, investment firms, even a genealogy company. Each time asking about my assets, my beneficiaries. Mrs. Lee saw him parked outside the house twice.

I had new locks installed and added cameras to the greenhouse. If something happens to me, the footage saves to the cloud. Password is your mother's maiden name plus your birth year.

Trust yourself, Clara. Your instincts have always been good, even when anxiety makes you doubt them. Don't let anyone convince you otherwise.

All my love, Margaret

P.S. - I kept journals too. Hidden in the greenhouse, behind the orchid fertilizer.

Sometimes writing things down is the only way to know they really happened.

Clara read it twice, then photographed it with her phone. She folded the letter carefully, placing it back inside the envelope.

When she returned, Julian and Krell were discussing investment strategies.

"Everything alright?" Julian asked.

"Fine."

"What did the letter say?"

"Personal things. Memories of my mother." The lie came easily. "She kept some of my mother's jewelry. Wanted to make sure I knew where to find it."

"That's thoughtful."

The rest of the meeting was paperwork. Signatures, initial here, sign there. Clara's hand cramped from writing her name so many times. Finally, Krell stood. "Again, my condolences. Margaret was a remarkable woman."

"You knew her well?" Clara asked.

"We'd worked together for fifteen years. She was . . . particular. Liked things documented properly." He paused. "She mentioned you often. Said you were a talented writer."

"She read all my drafts."

"She was very proud." Krell walked them to the door. "If you need anything, my direct line is on the card."

In the elevator, Julian was quiet. Clara could feel tension radiating from him like heat.

Once they were in the parking garage, he spoke.

"Two-point-eight million."

"It doesn't feel real."

"It's real." He opened her door. "We could invest it properly, live off the returns. Never worry about anything again."

We. Clara noticed the pronoun as she slid into the passenger seat.

During the drive home, Julian kept glancing at her. "You seem different today."

"Different how?"

"More focused. Less . . . scattered."

"Maybe the shock is wearing off."

"Maybe. Or maybe you didn't take your medication this morning."

"What medication?"

"The ones I—" He stopped. "Never mind. I'm thinking of something else."

They drove in silence for several minutes. Then Julian's phone rang through the car's Bluetooth. He looked at the display: David Morrison.

"I should take this."

"Put it on speaker. I'd like to hear the client who monopolizes your weekends."

Julian hesitated, then answered. "Julian Thorne."

Silence. Then a dial tone.

"Must have lost connection," Julian said. "Cell towers are terrible out here."

Clara pulled out her phone. Full bars. She didn't comment.

At home, Julian disappeared into his office immediately. "Market research," he said. "Need to check the Asian markets."

Clara stood in the kitchen, staring at the coffee maker. The bag of special blend sat beside it. She opened it, inhaling. Definitely coffee. She took a photo of the label, then googled the brand.

No results.

She tried variations of the name, checked Amazon, specialty coffee sites. Nothing.

A sound from outside caught her attention. On the back porch, Mavis was setting out fresh water for Stanley.

Clara walked over, needing normal conversation with someone who didn't make her question reality.

"How are you holding up, dear?" Mavis asked.

"It's been hard."

"I can imagine. Margaret was such a lovely woman. Stanley, say hello to Clara." The parrot tilted his head, studying her. "Hello, Clara. Pretty girl. Pretty, pretty girl."

"That's new," Clara said.

"Oh, he's been full of new phrases lately. Picked them up from somewhere." Mavis shook her head. "This morning he kept saying 'August first' over and over. Like a broken record."

Stanley ruffled his feathers. Then, in a man's voice: "She's more stable than expected."

A woman's voice: "Increase the dose."

"Television," Mavis said apologetically. "He must be picking up some medical drama now. You know how they love their deadlines and emergencies. And I must admit, I do love those shows."

"Must be," Clara agreed.

But as she walked back to her house, she couldn't shake the feeling that the voices were from real people.

That evening, Julian cooked supper. Salmon again.

"I've been thinking," he said, plating the fish. "You should consider power of attorney. Just temporarily. While you're dealing with grief."

"I can manage."

"Can you?" He set the plate in front of her. "You couldn't remember your PIN at the grocery store yesterday."

She didn't remember going to the grocery store yesterday. "That's different."

"Is it? Clara, I'm trying to help. This is a lot of money. There will be taxes, investment decisions, legal documents. Let me handle it while you focus on healing."

"I said I can manage."

"Fine. But when you make mistakes, and you will, remember I offered to help."

After supper, Clara went to bed early, claiming a headache. She retrieved her journal from inside the old shoebox and wrote quickly:

Tuesday, July 11th

Margaret changed her will six days before she died. She knew someone was watching her.

Greenhouse has cameras. Check footage.

Julian knows things he shouldn't—the way to Krell's office, estate law details.

Morrison's phone disconnected? Wrong number? Or something else?

Coffee brand doesn't exist online.

She stopped writing. The simplest explanation was usually the right one. And the simplest explanation was that she was falling apart.

Margaret had been elderly, probably anxious about normal things like utility scams. The coffee could be from some local roaster. Morrison's call could have been a legitimate disconnect. Julian could have researched estate law to help her. Or she could be right about everything.

The bedroom door opened. Clara shoved the journal under her pillow.

"Headache better?" Julian asked.

"A little."

He sat on the edge of the bed, held out two white pills and a glass of water. "These will help."

"What are they?"

"Just ibuprofen."

Clara took the pills, placed them on her tongue, accepted the water. She'd gotten better at this.

"Let me see," Julian said.

"What?"

"Open your mouth. I want to make sure you swallowed them."

She opened her mouth, lifting her tongue slightly, praying the pills stayed hidden in her cheek.

Julian peered at her mouth, then nodded. "Good. Sleep well."

After he left, she retrieved the shoebox from the closet, lifted out the old receipts and warranty cards she'd placed on top as camouflage. Her journal went in first, then Margaret's letter, carefully folded. The pills in their tissue she tucked into a small plastic bag she'd hidden there earlier—evidence, maybe, if she ever needed it. Or proof of her paranoia if she was wrong about everything.

She replaced the papers on top and slid the box back behind her winter boots. Julian had already found one hiding spot. She'd have to be more careful.

Outside, Stanley was practicing his repertoire. She heard him cycle through doorbell sounds and phone rings.

Then, clear as day, in a man's voice. Julian's?: "She won't suspect anything."

But when Clara listened closer, she realized it could have been anyone's voice. The night distorted things, made them seem significant. Maybe Mavis was right. Maybe it was just television.

She lay back and tried to decide which was worse: being paranoid or being right

5

WEDNESDAY, JULY 12TH

Dr. Alana Graves's office was less a place of healing and more a statement of minimalist wealth. The chairs were stark white leather, the desk a slab of polished chrome, and the only art on the wall was a single, massive abstract painting of chaotic black lines on a white canvas. It felt less like a doctor's office and more like a high-end art gallery.

Clara sat on the edge of one of the chairs, her hands clasped tightly in her lap. Julian sat beside her, his posture the perfect picture of concerned devotion. He had one hand resting on her back, a gesture that was meant to look supportive but felt like an intrusion.

Dr. Graves sat opposite them, a manila folder with Clara's name on it placed squarely in the center of her desk. She was sharp and angular, dressed in an impeccably tailored black suit, her dark hair pulled back.

"Clara," she began. "Julian tells me you've been under a great deal of stress lately. The loss of your aunt must have been a terrible shock."

"It has been."

"He also mentioned you've been experiencing some... confusion. Memory gaps. A feeling of paranoia, perhaps?" Dr. Graves's pen hovered over a blank page on her notepad.

"I've been having trouble sleeping, sometimes sleeping too much," Clara said, choosing her words carefully. "And Julian has been trying to help."

Julian squeezed her shoulder gently. "She's been forgetting things, Doctor. Important things. Appointments. Conversations. She's convinced herself that I'm . . . well, that I'm trying to harm her."

Dr. Graves made her first note. "Clara, your husband provided me with your medical history. You have a documented anxiety disorder, for which you previously sought treatment with a Dr. Kaminski."

"I did," Clara said. "She helped me develop coping strategies. I haven't had a serious episode in years."

"And yet, here we are," Dr. Graves said. "It's not uncommon for significant trauma, like the death of a loved one, to trigger a relapse. Sometimes, the old coping strategies are no longer sufficient. Julian mentioned you've developed a fixation on a neighbor's parrot, believing it's recording evidence of some kind."

Clara felt the anxiety returning. To say it out loud in this white room felt like an act of insanity. "The parrot mimics things it hears. It's repeated . . . conversations."

"Conversations you believe are evidence of a conspiracy against you?" Dr. Graves asked.

"I . . ." Clara looked at Julian, at his mask of sadness, and then back at the doctor's cool gaze. It was a perfect trap. Anything she said would be twisted, documented, and filed away as a symptom. "I know how it sounds."

"How it sounds is not as important as how it feels to you, Clara. These feelings of persecution are very real *to you*, and that's what we need to address."

The doctor's tone shifted from analytical to prescriptive. "I believe a mild antipsychotic would be beneficial. It will help quiet the intrusive, paranoid thoughts and allow your mind to rest and heal from the trauma. It will also help with the memory issues, which are often a symptom of an overactive, anxious mind."

She scribbled on a prescription pad. "I'm starting you on a low dose. We'll see how you respond, and we can adjust as needed." She tore the page off and handed it not to Clara, but to Julian.

"Have this filled immediately," she said to him. "And ensure she takes it as prescribed. Consistency is key." She then turned her gaze back to Clara. "Your husband is being remarkably patient, Clara. But this is a serious condition. We need to get it under control before it escalates."

The evening settled over the house, but it brought no peace. The meeting with Dr. Graves had been exactly what Clara had feared: a clinical confirmation of her own insanity, signed, sealed, and delivered with a prescription. That was why, when Julian had brought her the two white pills after supper, claiming they were for the "stress of the day," she had performed the most convincing swallow of her life.

Now, she lay awake and alone in the darkness. She pretended to sleep. The bedside clock glowed 11:47 PM. Julian thought she was unconscious, knocked out by the pills now safely tucked in a tissue inside the old shoebox.

She could hear his voice downstairs, a muffle from his office.

She forced herself to remain still, fighting the instinct to run.

Clara slipped out of bed, her movements silent on the thick bedroom carpet. She crept to the door, pressing her ear against the wood. Julian's voice grew clearer as she reached the top of the stairs.

"The first appointment went exactly as we planned," he was saying into the phone. "She's completely boxed in. Thinks the parrot is her only witness." He laughed, a cruel sound.

A pause.

"I agree, she's building a tolerance to the coffee. We need to increase the dosage. And you were right, we need a public incident. Something with witnesses."

Another pause.

"Yes, the paradoxical reaction. Agitation, aggression . . . perfect for documentation. Let's plan on Saturday. The farmer's market. That will give the new medication time to take hold."

Clara gripped the banister. The stairs creaked under her weight as she shifted, a sound no louder than a sigh, but in the quiet house, it was a gunshot.

Julian's voice stopped abruptly.

"I have to go," he said quickly.

Clara retreated to the bedroom, but not fast enough. Julian appeared in the doorway, silhouetted by the hall light.

"You're awake." It wasn't a question

6

THURSDAY, JULY 13

CLARA WOKE WITH HER tongue stuck to the roof of her mouth. The bedroom tilted when she tried to sit up. Whatever Dr. Graves had prescribed was stronger than anything she'd taken before; even the small amount that had absorbed before she'd vomited the pills left her feeling like she was moving through wet cement.

Julian's side of the bed was already cold. A note on his pillow: *Early client meeting. Drink your coffee. Take your medication. I'll know if you don't. Love you.*

That last line felt more like a threat than affection.

She made her way downstairs, gripping the banister. The coffee waited in her cup, still warm. She carried it to the sink and poured it out. From the kitchen window, she could see Mavis's house. Stanley's cage sat empty on the porch.

Clara climbed back upstairs, each step an effort. The shoebox was where she'd left it, though the papers on top were arranged differently. Her journal fell open to her latest entry, the handwriting barely recognizable as her own.

Then she noticed something else, an entry she did not remember making:

I keep thinking everyone is against me. Julian is so patient but I see plots everywhere. Maybe Dr. Graves is right. Maybe I need more help than I thought.

Sometimes I think about hurting myself. The thoughts come often. Would anyone miss me?

Clara photographed the pages. Evidence of what? Her own deterioration? Or Julian's manipulation?

She tucked everything back into the shoebox, arranging the papers exactly as she'd found them. Then she called Julian's office.

"Thorne Financial Advisory," his assistant said.

"Hi, Melissa. It's Clara. Could you tell Julian I'm going shopping for funeral thank-you cards? I'll have my phone if he needs me."

"Of course, Mrs. Thorne. I'll let him know as soon as he's out of his meeting."

Clara dressed, choosing jeans and a simple blouse, nothing that required complicated buttons or zippers. Her fingers felt clumsy from the medication residue. She missed the sleeve hole twice before managing to get her arm through. In the bathroom, she splashed cold water on her cheeks and applied concealer under her eyes.

She grabbed her keys and headed for her SUV, gripping the railing as she descended the porch steps. The world had a slight lag to it, as if everything moved a half-second behind when she turned her head.

She did stop at the stationery store first, establishing an alibi, but had to park crooked in the space, her depth perception off. Inside, she focused hard on acting normal, selecting thankyou cards while the clerk watched with concern.

"Are you feeling alright, hon?" the woman asked.

"Just tired. My aunt recently passed away."

"Oh, I'm so sorry."

The drive to Margaret's estate took longer than normal. Clara focused on her lane, hands at ten and two, checking her speed constantly because she couldn't trust her perception. Twice she drifted toward the shoulder and had to correct. A horn blared when she took a turn too wide.

She parked down the road, behind a stand of pine trees, not wanting her SUV visible from the house in case Julian had someone watching the property. Her impaired driving made her extra cautious, the last thing she needed was to explain to anyone why she was here when she'd told Julian's assistant she was shopping.

The walk to the house took five minutes, though it felt longer with her unsteady gait. She kept to the tree line at first, then followed Margaret's gravel driveway. The Victorian mansion looked exactly as it had two weeks ago when she'd last visited Margaret, except now weeds crept into the rose beds.

Mail overflowed from the box—sympathy cards mixed with junk mail and bills. If Mrs. Lee was still keeping her cleaning schedule, she'd handle it when she arrived. The accumulated mail suggested no one had been here since at least Sunday. Clara left it untouched, not wanting to leave evidence of her visit in case Julian somehow checked.

The spare key was still under the third orchid pot on the front porch. Clara let herself in.

The house smelled of the kind of staleness that comes when no one opens windows or brews coffee or brings life into spaces.

Clara went straight to the staircase. The third step down had a dark stain on the edge. She knelt, examining it. Could be blood. Could be anything.

She continued to the greenhouse, accessed through the back of the house. Margaret's sanctuary, filled with orchids in every color. The camera Margaret had mentioned in her letter was there, mounted in the corner, but it faced the wall.

Behind the fertilizer bags, exactly where Margaret's letter had promised, Clara found three journals. She opened the most recent:

June 3rd - Clara's husband visited again today. Third time this month. Always when Clara's not with him. Asks about my health, my daily routines. Today he asked about the stairs— did I ever have trouble with them? Such an odd question.

June 15th - J. Thorne came by. Wanted to discuss Clara's "fragile mental state." Claimed she'd been having episodes. I've seen no evidence of this. Clara seems happy, if anything. Why is he trying to convince me she's unwell?

June 28th - That man was here again. This time asking about my will, if I have "everything in order." The presumption! I'm changing my will tomorrow. Clara needs protection from him.

July 1st - Called Nathan Callahan. He's a good boy, always looked out for Clara. Told him my concerns. He promised to watch out for her.

July 7th - I'm frightened. Installed cameras in greenhouse. If something happens to me, it wasn't an accident.

Clara photographed each page, then heard a car door slam. She peeked through the greenhouse glass. Mrs. Lee's old Chevy was in the driveway.

The housekeeper entered through the back door, carrying cleaning supplies. She gasped when she saw Clara.

"Oh! Miss Clara! You scared me half to death." Mrs. Lee pressed a hand to her chest. "I didn't expect anyone."

"I needed to see where it happened."

Mrs. Lee's voice broke. "I shouldn't have left her alone that weekend. But she insisted she'd be fine."

"It's not your fault."

"I found her Sunday morning." Mrs. Lee set down her supplies. "She was at the bottom of the stairs, but . . ." She hesitated.

"What?"

"The position was wrong. Like she'd been . . . arranged. And her slippers were still upstairs. She never walked those stairs without her slippers. Bad arthritis in her feet."

"Did you tell the police?"

"They said old people get confused. Middle of the night, probably forgot her slippers." Mrs. Lee glanced toward the stairs. "Your husband was here several times. Miss Margaret didn't like it, but she didn't want to upset you. He was always asking questions."

A sound from outside made them both freeze. Through the window, a black sedan pulled into the driveway.

"I need to hide." Clara ducked into the dining room, pressing herself against the wall.

The doorbell rang. She heard Mrs. Lee's footsteps, then the door opening.

"Yes?"

"I'm looking for Mrs. Thorne. Her vehicle is parked down the road."

Clara stepped into the doorway where he could see her.

"Mrs. Thorne. My employer would like me to remind your husband about his obligations."

"I don't know what you're talking about."

"Five hundred thousand dollars. August first. Tell him Viktor doesn't give extensions. And Mrs. Thorne? Your husband's debt becomes your debt if something happens to him. That's how these things work."

He walked back to his sedan and drove away.

Mrs. Lee watched from the doorway. "Miss Clara, do you know that man?"

"Never saw him before." Clara glanced toward the window, half-expecting to see the sedan still there.

"I have to go."

She took the back path through the woods until she reached her car. She drove to downtown Saugatuck, needing time to think before facing Julian. The coffee shop was crowded with summer tourists. She ordered tea—nothing that could be tampered with—and found a corner table.

"Clara?"

She looked up. Nate Callahan stood there in track pants and a Saugatuck High School Football t-shirt.

"Nate." Relief flooded through her at seeing a trustworthy face.

"Damn, Clara. You look—are you okay? You've lost weight. And your hands are shaking."

She looked down. Her hands were trembling against the paper cup.

"I'm fine."

"Bullshit." He pulled out the chair across from her. "What's he doing to you?"

The directness of the question almost broke her. "What do you mean?"

"Margaret called me two weeks ago. Said Julian had been coming around, asking strange questions about you. About your anxiety history, your mother's mental health. She didn't trust him, Clara."

"I'm glad she called you."

"We talked for an hour. She was scared. Said he was planning something." Nate leaned forward. "She changed her will because of him. Did you know that?"

Clara nodded.

"Look, I know we haven't been close since the wedding, but we've known each other since middle school. Something's wrong. I can see it."

She wanted to tell him everything—about the drugs, the gaslighting, and Stanley's mimicry. But how could she? It sounded insane even to her. "I'm just having a hard time."

"Give me your phone," Nate said.

Clara hesitated, then handed it over. He typed quickly.

"My cell," he said, showing her the new contact before giving the phone back. "Call me. Day or night, Clara. I mean it."

"Nate—"

"Something's not right here. Margaret knew it. I think you know it too."

After he left, Clara sat for another twenty minutes, staring at his number. Then she drove home, stopping first to hide Margaret's journals in her SUV's spare tire compartment.

Julian's BMW was in the driveway when she arrived. He was in the kitchen, preparing supper. The smell of salmon filled the house once more.

"There you are! How was shopping?"

She held up the bag of thank-you cards.

"Perfect. Very thoughtful." He stirred something on the stove. "Run into anyone interesting today?"

The question was casual, but Clara heard the edge underneath.

"Just tourists."

"Funny. Mrs. Lee called me. Said you were at Margaret's house. Said you seemed confused, disoriented."

Clara froze. Mrs. Lee had called him? "I needed to see where it happened."

"Without telling me?"

"I didn't think I needed permission."

Julian set down the spatula. "Dr. Graves called. She's concerned about you driving alone. These

56

medications can cause dissociative episodes. You might not even remember where you've been."

He pulled out his phone, showed her a video. Her SUV parked at Margaret's estate. Time stamp from today.

"Who took this?"

"Mrs. Lee was worried. Asked a neighbor to keep an eye out." He pocketed the phone.

"You were there for an hour, honey. Do you remember what you did for that whole hour?"

She did remember. Every minute. But an hour? It couldn't have been that long. And the video showed her SUV in the driveway, but she distinctly remembered parking down the road, walking up through the trees. Hadn't she? The certainty in his voice made her doubt her own memory.

"I was just walking through the house."

"For an hour? Alone? While on heavy psychiatric medication?" He turned the salmon. "Dr. Graves wants to increase your dose. She thinks you might be a danger to yourself."

"I'm not—"

"Clara." He turned to face her. "You went to a house where someone just died. You were confused, according to Mrs. Lee. You can't account for a full hour. This isn't normal behavior."

At supper, he watched her take her pills, checking her mouth thoroughly after she swallowed. She couldn't fake it this time. Within twenty minutes, the edges of the world began to soften.

"Tell me about your day," Julian said. "Where did you go after Margaret's house?"

"Coffee shop."

"Alone?"

The medication made it hard to lie. "Saw Nate."

"Nate Callahan? What did he want?"

"Just said hello. He was at the funeral."

"What else?"

"Nothing. Just . . . condolences."

Julian watched her for a long moment. "You should be careful around him. He's always had feelings for you. Might try to take advantage of your vulnerable state."

Through her medication fog, Clara wanted to laugh. Nate taking advantage? While Julian drugged her nightly?

After Julian helped her to bed, she fought to stay conscious. Through the door, she heard his voice on the phone:

"She went to the estate . . . Increase the dose tomorrow. We're running out of time."

A pause.

"Yes, the brunch with the Hendersons is all set for tomorrow. We'll get photos, a credit card receipt with her signature . . . more 'evidence' of a good day she won't be able to remember. We need to document these episodes. Build the narrative."

Another pause.

"Don't worry. By the time we're done, she won't know what's real."

Clara dragged herself to the window, needing fresh air. In the oak tree, Stanley perched like a small gray guardian.

Clara pressed her forehead against the cool glass, feeling like she was losing touch with reality.

But Margaret's journals were real. She'd written them weeks before Julian could have known about them. Those were still hidden in her car.

If she could just stay conscious long enough tomorrow to get them to someone who'd believe her. Someone like Nate.

The medication pulled her under before she could finish the thought, Stanley's voice following her into darkness: "The money's all mine. The money's all mine."

7

FRIDAY, JULY 14

Clara woke to unfamiliar wallpaper. Pale blue stripes instead of the cream walls of their bedroom. The guest room. Why was she in the guest room?

She sat up, head pounding, and looked down at herself. A navy dress she didn't recognize clung to her body. Her hair fell around her shoulders in soft, styled waves. When she raised a hand to touch it, the strands were damp at the roots.

The bedside clock read 1:47 PM.

She stood, gripping the nightstand as the room swayed. A foreign perfume clung to her skin. Her last memory was taking those pills after supper last night, then arguing with Julian about going to Dr. Graves. Everything after that was black.

Downstairs, Julian hummed in the kitchen. She could smell coffee and something sweet like pastries.

"There you are!" He said as she entered. "I was starting to worry. You said you wanted to lie down after brunch, but that was two hours ago."

"Brunch?"

"With the Hendersons. Tom and Linda?" He pulled out his phone, swiping to photos.

"You were wonderful, by the way. So articulate about your novel. Like your old self."

The photos showed her at Copper Rock, the upscale restaurant downtown. She sat beside a blonde woman, raising a mimosa to the camera.

"I don't remember any of this."

"You don't remember Linda complimenting your dress? You were so pleased; told her you'd bought it specially for the occasion."

Clara looked down at the navy dress again. "I've never seen this dress before."

He stepped closer, concerned. "These memory gaps are getting worse."

She backed away, needing space. Her purse sat on the counter. Inside, she found a receipt from Copper Rock, time-stamped 10:15 AM. Her signature on the credit card slip, close to her handwriting but the C in Clara was wrong.

Her phone showed sent messages she didn't remember typing:

Linda, thank you so much for the wonderful brunch! So lovely to finally meet you. Let's do it again soon! - Clara Time-stamped 12:45 PM.

"I need air," Clara said.

"Of course. But take your medication first." Julian produced the pill bottle. "Dr. Graves increased the dose this morning."

"This morning?"

"During your emergency session. You don't remember that either? Clara, this is serious. She's talking about more intensive treatment if these episodes continue."

Clara's hand went to her inner arm where she felt a small bandage. She peeled back the edge—a needle mark, like from a blood draw.

"What is this?"

"Blood work. Dr. Graves needed to check your medication levels." Julian shook out three pills instead of two. "Please. Just take them."

The doorbell saved her from responding.

Julian frowned. "Who could that be?"

He went to answer it. Clara heard voices as she moved to the hallway.

Nate stood in the doorway, wearing his coaching jacket.

"—just want to make sure she's okay," Nate was saying.

"She's fine." Julian blocked the doorway with his body.

"Clara?" Nate called over Julian's shoulder. "You called me at 3 AM. You were crying, asking for help. Then the line went dead."

Clara pulled out her phone. There it was in her call log: Nate Callahan, 3:13 AM, duration 47 seconds.

"I don't remember—"

"Of course you don't." Julian's voice hardened. "Because you were having an episode. Nate, I appreciate your concern, but Clara is getting professional help. Your involvement is just confusing her."

"Professional help?" Nate tried to see past Julian. "Clara, what's he talking about?"

"Show him the photos," Julian said to Clara. "From this morning. Show him how well you're doing."

Clara's hands remained at her sides. She couldn't bring herself to participate in this charade.

"Clara?" Julian said. "The photos?"

When she didn't move, Julian took the phone from her hand. "She's had a long day." He swiped to the brunch photos and held the screen toward Nate. "See? She was perfectly fine this morning. Socializing, laughing. Today was actually wonderful until you showed up."

"Clara, is this what you want?" Nate asked, looking directly at her, ignoring the phone Julian was practically pushing in his face.

Before she could answer, Julian stepped fully outside, closing the door behind him, leaving Clara in the hallway. She pressed her ear to the door.

"—need to stay away from my wife," Julian was saying. "She's fragile right now."

"Margaret was right about you."

"Margaret was an elderly woman with paranoid delusions. Now if you'll excuse me—"

Clara heard footsteps on the porch, then the door opened. Julian entered alone, but as he turned to close the door, she saw Nate still standing there. Their eyes met for a second, and Nate mouthed something. Then Julian shut the door firmly.

"He means well," Julian said, "but he's always had feelings for you. It clouds his judgment."

Clara went to the window, watching Nate walk to his truck. As he passed their mailbox, he paused, pretending to tie his shoe while slipping something under the stack of mail.

"I need to check the mail," Clara said.

"I already got it."

"There might be sympathy cards. I should check."

"Clara—"

But she was already heading outside. The rain had picked up, soaking through her unfamiliar dress immediately. She opened the mailbox, finding grocery circulars. Underneath them, a small envelope with her name.

She took it, grabbing the junk mail as cover, and hurried back inside.

"Just circulars," she said, heading upstairs. "I need to change. This dress is soaked."

In the bathroom, door locked, she opened Nate's envelope. Inside was a photocopy of a journal entry in Margaret's handwriting:

June 28th - That man was here again asking about my will. I'm changing it tomorrow. Clara needs protection from him. I'm sending this to Nathan Callahan for safekeeping. If something happens to me, he'll know what to do.

Underneath, Nate had written: *She mailed this to me July 3rd. Call me from a pay phone.*

Clara hid the note temporarily under her jewelry box, then remembered—she'd hidden Margaret's journals in her car yesterday. She changed into jeans and a dry shirt, then headed back downstairs.

"I need something from my car," she told Julian as she put on her raincoat.

He barely glanced up from his tablet. "Hurry back. You still need to take your medication."

Clara grabbed her keys and went to her SUV. The rain provided cover as she popped the back hatch and lifted the floor panel to the spare tire compartment. The journals were gone.

In their place was a single document: a psychiatric evaluation form. *Patient exhibits severe paranoid delusions, recommends immediate inpatient treatment for her safety and the safety of others.* Dr. Graves's signature at the bottom. Dated today, though Clara hadn't seen Dr. Graves today. Had she?

She closed the trunk and went to Mavis's yard, desperate for something that made sense.

Stanley sat in his cage on the covered porch, protected from the rain.

"Clara!" Mavis opened her door. "Goodness, you're soaked. Come in, dear."

"I can't. I just—needed air."

Stanley tilted his head at her and spoke in a woman's voice: "The paperwork's ready. Just need one more incident."

"Oh, that bird," Mavis shook her head. "He's been repeating that all morning. Must be from those crazy TV programs." She studied Clara more closely. "You looked lovely this morning, by the way."

"This morning?"

"Yes, when you were walking to your car around eight. You even waved at me. That dress was so elegant."

"Eight?" But she'd woken a lot later than that.

"Just before your husband left. I saw you at the back of your SUV, took something out and walked over to the garbage bins with a bag. Spring cleaning?"

Clara remembered none of it. "Yes. Spring cleaning."

She hurried to the side of the road where the large plastic bin stood. She lifted the lid.

It was empty.

Of course. It was Friday. The garbage truck had already come this morning, its mechanical arm lifting and emptying the contents, erasing the evidence she hadn't even known she'd thrown away. The journals. Margaret's final words. Gone. Crushed and compacted and on their way to a landfill. A wave of despair washed over her.

Back inside, Julian waited in the kitchen with water and three pills.

"We need to talk about those journals," Clara said.

"What journals?"

"Margaret's journals. They were in my car."

"Honey, what are you talking about?"

"I hid them in my spare tire compartment yesterday. Now they're gone."

Julian's face shifted to deep concern. "Clara, you're scaring me. Should we call Dr. Graves?"

"They were there! Margaret wrote about you visiting her, asking about her will—"

"Clara, stop." He pulled out his phone, swiping to something. "I installed security cameras. For our protection." He turned the screen toward her. "This is from this morning."

Clara watched herself on video, walking to her SUV at 8:07 AM in the navy dress. She opened the hatch, removed something from the spare tire compartment, put it in a garbage bag, then threw it in the outdoor trash bin.

"You said they were 'evidence of your paranoia' and you wanted a fresh start," Julian said gently. "Don't you remember?"

The video was clear. It was definitely her. But she had no memory of it. None.

"I think we need to see Dr. Graves now," Julian said. "This is escalating."

"No—"

"Clara, you're having blackouts. You're inventing memories. You called Nate at 3 AM. This isn't normal grief anymore."

He picked up his phone, dialing. "Dr. Graves? It's Julian. Yes, she's having another episode. Can we come now?"

Clara tried to grab the phone, but he turned away.

"Thank you. We'll be right there." He ended the call. "Get your coat."

"I'm not going."

"You are." His voice turned cold. "Either you come voluntarily, or I call for help. Your choice."

She thought about running, but where would she go? He'd already convinced everyone she was having a breakdown. Even Nate couldn't help her now, Julian had neutralized him.

In the car, Julian engaged the child locks. At a red light, he forced the three pills into her hand.

"Take them."

"No."

"Clara, I'm trying to help you. Please don't make this harder."

She dry-swallowed the pills, showing him her empty mouth when he demanded it. The medication worked fast. By the time they reached Dr. Graves's office, everything had taken on an underwater quality.

"She's getting worse," she heard Julian tell Dr. Graves. "The memory gaps, the paranoia about journals that don't exist."

"This is consistent with what we discussed," Dr. Graves said. "The blood work confirms she's been inconsistent with her medication."

Blood work. The bandage on her arm. When had they drawn blood?

"Tomorrow," Dr. Graves was saying. "Public setting, multiple witnesses. The farmer's market would be ideal."

"She loves the farmer's market," Julian said.

Clara tried to speak, but her tongue felt thick. Tomorrow was her last day of freedom. After whatever they had planned at the farmer's market, she'd be locked away, and Julian would have everything.

At home, Julian helped her to the bedroom. "You need rest."

When Julian left, she retrieved the shoebox from behind her winter boots. The journal was there, but as she flipped through it, she found forged entries. She needed a new hiding place. She tucked the journal inside her shirt, pressing it against her stomach and rushed to the bathroom.

First, she wedged her journal vertically into the narrow gap between the toilet tank and the wall, where it would not be visible unless someone specifically looked. Then she dropped to her knees beside the toilet, reaching behind it where the wall met the floor. Using her lipstick, she wrote on the baseboard in small letters: *July 14 - He's taking me to commit me.*

The toilet tank hid both pieces of evidence from casual view—Julian would have to get on the floor and look behind the toilet to see them.

Julian's footsteps stopped outside the door. "Clara? You okay in there?"

She flushed the toilet and stood, gripping the sink. "Just feeling sick."

"Let's get you to bed."

As consciousness slipped away, she heard Stanley through the window, practicing his newest phrase over and over: "The money's all mine. The money's all mine. The money's all mine."

8

SATURDAY, JULY 15

CLARA WOKE WITH HER mouth dry as cotton; the new normal. Through the fog, fragments of overheard conversation surfaced about the farmer's market.

Julian's whistling drifted up from the kitchen. That same Sinatra tune he always chose when things were going his way. "Fly Me to the Moon" had become the soundtrack to her destruction.

She forced herself upright. The bedside clock read 7:23 AM. The farmer's market opened at nine. Whatever Julian had planned, she had less than two hours to prepare.

In the bathroom, she knelt carefully beside the toilet, checking behind it. Her lipstick message was still there. At least that evidence remained, though who would ever look for it?

Downstairs, Julian had set the kitchen table like a stage with fresh flowers and cloth napkins. He looked up from his tablet.

"Morning, beautiful. Big day today."

"Is it?" Clara kept her voice neutral as she sat down.

"The farmer's market. You've been talking about wanting to go for weeks." He set a cup of coffee in front of her. "Drink up while it's hot. That special blend works best warm."

She brought the cup to her lips, pretending to drink.

"Delicious," she said, setting the cup down.

"You seem better this morning."

"I feel a little better."

"Good. Because you need to take these before we go." He placed four white pills beside her cup. "Dr. Graves increased the dose, remember? After yesterday's episode."

Clara stared at the pills. "No."

"Clara, we talked about this."

"I don't want them. They make me foggy."

"Honey." He leaned forward. "Do you remember what Dr. Kaminski said about medication resistance? How it was one of your patterns?"

Dr. Kaminski had said that, years ago. "That was different—"

"Was it? You fought taking anxiety medication then too. You were convinced it was changing you, making you someone else." Julian said. "And then when you finally stayed on it consistently, you got so much better. You said so yourself at our wedding, how grateful you were that you'd pushed through that resistance."

"This isn't the same."

"Isn't it?" He reached across the table, not quite touching her hand. "Clara, think about what you're saying. You believe I'm drugging you. That's exactly the kind of paranoid thought Dr. Kaminski warned about. Remember? She said stress could trigger those patterns again."

Clara's certainty wavered. Dr. Kaminski had warned her about catastrophic thinking, about her tendency to spiral into paranoid interpretations when anxious.

"Margaret just died," Julian continued. "You're grieving. You inherited money you never expected. That's enormous stress. Is it really so strange that your old patterns would resurface?"

"But the coffee tastes—"

"Different? It's a new brand. An expensive one, actually. I thought it might help with your anxiety." He pulled out the bag, showed her the label again. "Adaptogenic blend. Look it up later if you want. Sixty dollars a pound."

Clara stared at the bag, the same one he had shown her before. "Margaret's death. The timing—"

"Honey, she was eighty-three. She'd been complaining about those stairs for years." His voice dropped. "Do you really think I murdered your aunt? Listen to yourself. Does that sound rational?"

When he said it out loud like that, it sounded insane. "The inheritance—"

"That you're trying to make into something sinister. Clara, I make good money. We don't need Margaret's estate. I'm trying to help you manage it because you're overwhelmed." He sat back. "But if you really think I'm some kind of monster plotting against you . . ."

He pulled out his phone.

"What are you doing?"

"Calling Dr. Graves. If you truly believe your husband is trying to harm you, then you're having paranoid delusions and need immediate psychiatric help."

"Julian, stop—"

"No, if you really believe what you're saying, then you're in crisis." He showed her the screen, Dr. Graves's number pulled up. "She has admitting privileges at Northwood Pines. They can keep you safe while we figure out what's happening with your mind."

"I don't need to be hospitalized."

"Then take your medication. Trust the process. Trust me." His thumb hovered over the call button. "Or I make this call, because a wife who thinks her husband is poisoning her is clearly having a psychiatric emergency."

The logic felt like a trap closing around her. Either she was paranoid and needed help, or she wasn't paranoid but had to act like she was wrong to avoid being committed.

"Clara, I love you. I've been nothing but patient through all of this—your confusion, your memory gaps, your accusations. Do you have any idea how much it hurts to have your wife look at you with suspicion? To be treated like a villain when all I'm trying to do is help?"

Tears pricked her eyes. What if he was right? What if grief and stress had triggered her old patterns? The alternative, that her husband of three months was systematically destroying her, seemed impossible when she looked at his concerned face.

"I'm sorry," she whispered.

"Take your medication. Please. For both of us."

Clara placed all four pills on her tongue and swallowed them with water. This time, she didn't try to hide any.

"Thank you." Julian came around the table, kissed her forehead. "I know it's hard. But Dr. Graves says the therapeutic dose needs to build up. You'll feel more like yourself soon."

"I feel like I'm losing myself."

"That's the illness talking. Not you." He squeezed her shoulder gently. "Go get dressed. The fresh air at the market will help."

Upstairs, Clara stared at herself in the bathroom mirror. Her own thoughts felt like enemies now. Every suspicion could be paranoia. Every doubt could be illness. Maybe Julian was right. Maybe she was sick. Or maybe that was exactly what he wanted her to think.

The medication was already starting to work as she turned on the shower. The hot water helped momentarily, sharpening her focus. She had maybe thirty minutes before the full effects hit.

She dressed quickly—jeans, a simple blue blouse, and flat shoes she wouldn't trip in. Everything chosen for function, not fashion. She blow-dried her hair halfway, leaving it damp.

"We need to leave soon," Julian called from downstairs.

Clara made her way to her small office, a converted third bedroom. Her laptop sat closed on the desk, her detective novel notebook beside it. Through the window, she could see Stanley preening on Mavis's porch.

She opened her laptop, fingers already clumsy on the keyboard. The password took two tries. Her manuscript was open, showing last accessed at 3:47 AM—when she'd been unconscious. She checked the document history. Multiple sessions she didn't remember, all during her blackout periods.

Her browser history showed searches she'd never made: "signs of schizophrenia," "paranoid delusions in women," "do I have psychosis quiz," "voluntary psychiatric commitment Michigan."

In her email drafts, a message to her editor: *I need to take an indefinite break for mental health reasons. I'm getting help, but the book will be delayed. Maybe permanently.*

Another draft to her college friends: *I've been struggling with paranoid thoughts. Julian is getting me help. Please don't be alarmed if you don't hear from me for a while.*

"Clara?" Julian called from downstairs. "We need to leave in twenty minutes."

She grabbed her purse, and checked her photos. The gallery was empty. Every picture from the last two weeks—gone. The screenshots of medication searches, the photos of journal pages, Margaret's letter. Even the Recently Deleted folder had been cleared.

While she was unconscious, Julian must have used her thumb to unlock the phone and erased everything.

"Clara? We need to go."

She descended the stairs, gripping the railing. Julian waited by the door, car keys in hand, looking every inch the devoted husband in his Saturday casuals.

"You look lovely. Ready?"

The drive to the farmer's market took fifteen minutes. Julian chatted pleasantly about vendors, weather, and plans for the garden. Clara responded minimally, concentrating on fighting the medication's effects.

The market bustled with Saturday shoppers. Julian's hand settled on her lower back, steering her through the crowds. He stopped at the honey stand first.

"Clara loves your wildflower honey," he told the vendor, a woman Clara recognized but couldn't name through the medication fog. "Don't you, honey?"

"Yes."

"She's been having a tough time lately," Julian continued. "Her aunt passed. She's been very confused."

The vendor offered condolences. Julian bought two jars, then guided Clara to the next stand—orchids. The woman there smiled in recognition.

"Mrs. Thorne! Haven't seen you in weeks."

"She's been unwell," Julian answered for her. "Grief does terrible things to the mind."

As they moved through the market, Julian repeated variations of this narrative to every vendor, every acquaintance they encountered. Clara was grieving. Clara was confused. Clara was getting help.

At the bakery stand, Julian bought her a cinnamon roll. "Your favorite," he said loudly. "You had three of these last week, remember?"

Clara had no memory of being at the market last week. "I don't—"

"Of course you don't remember." His voice carried perfectly to the surrounding shoppers. "You've been having these episodes. That's why we're seeing Dr. Graves."

He tore off a piece of the roll, holding it to her lips. "Eat something. You forgot breakfast again."

She hadn't forgotten—he'd never offered breakfast. But several people were watching now, seeing her husband's patient care, her confused resistance.

"I'm not hungry."

"Clara, you have to eat. You forgot supper last night too." He turned to the baker with an apologetic smile. "She's been skipping meals. The doctor says it's part of her condition."

Clara wanted to scream that she'd eaten salmon last night, again, and that he'd watched her eat it, but the medication made her thoughts move like thick syrup. By the time she formulated the words, the moment had passed.

They continued through the market. At each stop, Julian built his narrative. Clara was sick. Clara needed help. Poor Julian, so devoted, so patient.

Near the flower stand, Clara saw a familiar face, Linda Henderson from the supposed brunch she couldn't remember.

The woman waved enthusiastically. "Clara! Twice in one week. How lovely!"

"She doesn't remember seeing you," Julian said quickly. "The memory issues are getting worse."

"But we just had brunch yesterday." Linda looked concerned. "Clara, you sent me that sweet thank-you text."

Clara stared at her. "I don't remember any brunch."

Linda's face shifted from concern to alarm. She glanced at Julian, who shook his head sadly.

"The doctor says it's dissociative episodes," he said. "She loses whole chunks of time."

More people had stopped to listen. Clara recognized faces from their neighborhood, from Julian's office, from the coffee shop downtown. All watching her confusion, her inability to remember a brunch multiple people had witnessed.

"I need to go home," Clara said.

"Of course." Julian's arm went around her shoulders. "Let's get you home. You're having another episode."

As he guided her through the crowd, she heard the whispers starting. *Poor thing. Mental breakdown. So young. Lucky she has him.*

In the car, Julian was silent until they pulled into their driveway. Then he turned to her. "That was difficult, wasn't it? You really don't remember seeing Linda yesterday." His voice was sympathetic. "Clara, when multiple people confirm something happened and you have no memory of it . . . honey, that's serious."

Clara watched his face, searching for cracks in the mask. Finding none.

"I recorded some of it to show Dr. Graves," he continued, pulling out his phone. "She needs to see these episodes to help you properly."

Clara watched herself on the small screen—confused, defensive, paranoid-looking. The perfect picture of mental illness. "I look crazy."

"You look sick. There's a difference." He pocketed the phone. "But we're going to get you help. Dr. Graves is coming by later to discuss treatment options."

"Why today? Why the market?"

"I didn't plan for you to have an episode, Clara. I thought getting out might help." He sighed. "But maybe we need to consider that outpatient treatment isn't enough anymore. Maybe you need more intensive help."

The threat was there, wrapped in concern. But the mask never slipped.

"Let's go inside. You need to rest."

In the house, Clara headed straight for the bathroom, locking the door. She ran cold water, splashing it on her face.

Through the window, she could hear Stanley squawking. She had to get to Mavis. Had to get help. But when she opened the bathroom door, Julian stood in the hallway.

"Dr. Graves is coming by," he said. "We need to discuss today's episode."

"I don't want to see her."

"It's not optional anymore." He guided her to the living room, his grip firm on her elbow. "Sit. She'll be here in twenty minutes."

Clara sank into the couch, the medication making resistance feel impossible. Julian sat across from her, scrolling through his phone. She could see him reviewing the market video, making notes.

A knock at the door made her jump. But it wasn't Dr. Graves, it was Mavis, holding a covered plate.

"So sorry to interrupt," Mavis said when Julian answered. "I made too many cookies. Thought Clara might enjoy some."

"How thoughtful." Julian's voice was ice. "But Clara's not feeling well."

"Oh dear. Is it those episodes again?" Mavis peered around him. "That elegant woman with the dark hair mentioned Clara's been having troubles. Such a dedicated doctor, making house calls."

Julian shifted his weight, blocking more of the doorway. "Thank you for the cookies."

But Mavis wasn't done. "Stanley's been so chatty today. Picked up the funniest phrases. Would you like to hear?"

Before Julian could refuse, Stanley's voice carried clearly from next door: "The money's all mine. She won't remember anything. August first. August first."

"Television," Mavis laughed. "He must be picking up some crime show."

"We need to go." Julian practically pushed Mavis out, shutting the door firmly.

Through her medication haze, Clara felt a spark of hope. Mavis had noticed Dr. Graves visiting. Stanley was recording everything. If she could just stay conscious enough to—

The doorbell rang again. This time it was Dr. Graves, dressed in a black suit. She entered without greeting Clara, speaking directly to Julian.

"I reviewed the video. Perfect. Multiple witnesses to her dissociative state and paranoid ideation."

"She denied remembering the Henderson brunch entirely," Julian added.

"Excellent." Dr. Graves finally looked at Clara, but as if she were a specimen, not a person. "How much of the medication is she taking?"

"Four this morning, plus the coffee. She seems more resistant lately."

"We'll need to increase it for tomorrow." Dr. Graves pulled out a prescription pad, then reached into her medical bag. "I'll write for an injectable. More reliable."

"Tomorrow?" Clara forced herself to focus.

"Your evaluation," Dr. Graves said coolly. "To determine if you need inpatient treatment. Based on today's public episode and Julian's documentation, I think we both know the outcome."

She handed Julian two prefilled syringes. "Tonight, before bed. One should be sufficient, but I've included a backup. This particular combination can cause paradoxical agitation in some patients. She might become aggressive or have urges to self-harm. If that happens, call 911 immediately. Tell them she's under psychiatric care and needs transport to Northwood Pines specifically. I'll admit her and control her treatment plan, medications, lab work, everything."

Julian nodded.

"When she becomes agitated we'll have witnesses—the EMTs, police if necessary—to her dangerous behavior." Dr. Graves glanced at Clara. "The medication I've prepared makes that reaction likely. Consider it insurance."

They continued discussing her as if she weren't there. Commitment procedures. Power of attorney. Asset transfer timelines. Clara tried to memorize every word, but fragments kept slipping away.

"We should administer the first dose now," Dr. Graves said, pulling a prefilled syringe from her medical bag. "I'll show you the proper technique."

"Now?" Julian glanced at Clara. "She's already sedated."

"This is a different formulation. Longer-acting. It will ensure she's manageable through tomorrow's evaluation." Dr. Graves approached Clara. "Watch carefully. You'll need to do this yourself tonight."

Clara tried to pull away. "No, please—"

"Hold her arm," Dr. Graves told Julian. "Firmly, but don't leave bruises."

Julian's hands pressed Clara's arm against the couch.

"Upper arm is best, but the thigh or abdomen will work if necessary." Dr. Graves swabbed Clara's arm with alcohol. "Insert at this angle, quick and smooth. Like this."

The needle went in with a sharp sting. Clara watched the clear liquid disappear into her arm.

"The key is confidence," Dr. Graves said, placing the syringe into bag. "Hesitation causes bruising. Questions from other medical staff. It's your turn tonight. Same spot, other arm. Then again in the morning."

"What if she resists or remembers our conversation?"

"She won't. Not after this dose." Dr. Graves watched Clara. "See? Already taking effect."

Clara felt the new medication spreading through her system.

"I should go," Dr. Graves said. "I have evening rounds."

"Let me walk you out." Julian gestured toward the front door.

Clara heard their footsteps move into the foyer, then stop. The front door didn't open. Instead, there was silence, then soft sounds—fabric rustling, a quiet sigh that was definitely not Julian's.

"Tomorrow night," Dr. Graves said with a soft, breathy tone. "After she's admitted."

"Your place?"

"Too risky. The Marriott downtown. I'll text you."

Another rustling sound, then what could only be a kiss—that specific quiet sound of lips parting.

"Two more weeks," Julian said. "Then we won't have to hide anymore."

"Assuming your creditor doesn't become impatient."

"He'll get his money. August first, as promised."

The front door opened then, and Dr. Graves's voice resumed its professional distance. "Call if there are any adverse reactions to the medication."

"Of course, Doctor."

Clara heard the door close, Julian's footsteps returning.

Julian stood over her. "You should rest. Big day tomorrow."

Clara let him help her to the bedroom, her legs barely cooperating. Each step required enormous concentration. The injection combined with the morning pills created a fog so thick she could barely hold a thought.

Once Julian left, she tried to fight the medication. She needed to warn someone. Nate. She needed to tell Nate but was unable.

As evening fell, Julian returned with soup.

She took a few sips, then "accidentally" knocked the bowl over. "I'm so sorry—"

"It's fine. You need your evening medication anyway."

He held out the syringe. "Dr. Graves says this is more effective."

"Please, no—"

"Clara, you're sick. This is for your own good." He prepared the injection site.

She tried to pull away, but he was stronger. The needle went into her arm.

"There. Now you'll rest properly."

As the injection took hold, dragging her toward unconsciousness, Clara heard her phone ring. Julian answered it.

"Clara can't come to the phone right now . . . No, she's resting. She had a difficult day . . . I don't think that's appropriate, Mr. Callahan . . . She needs space from people who encourage her delusions . . . If you call again, I'll consider it harassment."

The conversation ended. Then the phone rang again. Was it Nate calling back?

This time Julian declined the call. Clara heard him doing something with her phone. Was he changing settings or blocking Nate's number?

Through the window, Stanley was performing his evening repertoire. The last thing Clara heard before darkness claimed her was:

"The money's all mine. The money's all mine. The money's all mine."

Then nothing.

9

SUNDAY, JULY 16

CLARA WOKE TO A world that wouldn't stop spinning. Her biceps ached from the injections.

Julian's voice drifted up from the kitchen, talking on the phone. ". . . yes, Doctor. She's still sleeping. The second dose? Yes, just as you instructed."

He'd injected her while she slept.

She tried to sit up. The effort sent her rolling sideways, barely catching herself before falling off the bed. Her skin crawled with what felt like insects moving just beneath the surface. She felt exhausted and frantically restless at the same time.

Clara managed to stand, using the wall for support. Each step to the bathroom required enormous concentration. In the mirror, a stranger stared back—pupils blown wide, hair matted with sweat, hands trembling visibly.

She knelt beside the toilet, remembering. The journal. Her evidence. Right there, wedged between the tank and the wall. She reached behind, fingers scraping against porcelain, but her coordination was gone. Her hand knocked against the tank, too loud. She tried again, nearly falling forward, having to grip the sink to keep from collapsing.

"Clara?" Julian called from downstairs. "You okay up there?"

"Fine."

She couldn't retrieve the journal. Not like this. But it was there. Someone would find it. They had to.

Clara made her way downstairs, gripping the banister with both hands. The restlessness was getting worse; she needed to move, to do something with her hands.

Julian stood at the stove, spatula in hand. "Eggs?"

"Not hungry."

"You need to eat something."

She couldn't sit still. The medication made her pace the kitchen, five steps one way, five steps back. Her skin felt too tight.

"Please sit down," Julian said. "You're making me nervous."

"I can't. I need . . ." She didn't know what she needed. Her body wanted to run, to fight, to scream, even as the medicine made her muscles weak.

"I'll make toast," she said, needing to do something with her hands.

She pulled the bread from the cupboard, her shaking fingers struggling with the twist tie. The knife drawer was closer than the toaster. She pulled it open, grabbed the bread knife.

"Nate called again this morning," Julian said behind her. "Three times. I had to block his number."

Clara turned, still holding the knife. "Nate knows—"

"Knows what?" Julian stepped back dramatically. "Clara, put down the knife." She looked down, confused. She was just holding a bread knife. "I was making toast—"

"Put it DOWN!" He already had his phone in his hand, fingers flying across the screen.

"Please, honey, you're scaring me."

"Julian, I'm just—"

"Emergency? Yes, my wife is having a psychiatric emergency." He backed toward the doorway, phone pressed to his ear. "She's threatening me with a knife. She's under psychiatric care, Dr. Alana Graves, she's been having violent episodes."

"I'm not threatening you!" Clara set the knife on the counter, but her hands were shaking so badly it clattered against the granite. "I was making breakfast!"

"Please hurry," Julian continued into the phone. "She's very agitated. She's been medication non-compliant. The address is 423 Lakeshore Drive."

Clara stared at him. "Julian, please—"

"Stay back!" He held up a hand, though she hadn't moved. "The police are coming. They'll help you."

"I don't need help. I need you to stop—"

"Stop what? Stop trying to get you treatment? Stop caring that my wife is having a psychotic break?"

The sirens were already audible.

Two officers arrived within minutes—one male, older, with gray at his temples, and one female, younger, with her hand resting on her service weapon.

"We got a call about a domestic disturbance?" the male officer said.

"My wife." Julian's voice broke perfectly. "She's been having episodes. She's under Dr. Graves's care for severe mental illness, but she's been refusing her medication; sometimes taking too much."

Clara tried to stay still, but the agitation from the drugs made it impossible. She shifted from foot to foot, her hands clenching and unclenching.

"Ma'am, are you okay?" the female officer asked.

"I'm fine. My husband is lying—" The words came out slurred, her tongue too thick.

The officers exchanged glances. Clara saw herself through their eyes: dilated pupils, shaking hands, unable to stand still, words slurred. A knife on the counter behind her.

"She was holding it when I came in," Julian said, pointing to the knife. "Waving it around. She's been paranoid, thinking I'm trying to poison her."

Julian pulled out his phone, showing them something. "I've been documenting her episodes. This was yesterday at the farmer's market; multiple witnesses saw her having a dissociative episode."

The male officer watched the video while the female officer kept her eyes on Clara.

"Ma'am, are you taking any medications?" she asked.

"He's drugging me—"

"She's prescribed antipsychotics," Julian interrupted. "But she thinks they're poison. Classic paranoid delusion. Dr. Graves said this might happen, she recommended Northwood, Pines if Clara became violent."

"I'm not violent!" Clara's voice rose, and she immediately saw the officers tense.

"Please, you have to listen. Check the bathroom—"

"Ma'am, do you need to use the restroom?" the female officer asked.

"No! There's—" The words tangled in her mouth. "Evidence. He killed my aunt."

The officers exchanged another look.

"Her aunt died last week," Julian said softly. "A fall. Clara's been unable to process the grief. She's constructed this elaborate delusion that I murdered her for money."

"It's not a delusion!"

"Ma'am, we're going to need you to come with us," the male officer said. "For a psychiatric evaluation. It's for your safety and others."

"No, please—"

"This can go easy or hard," he continued. "But either way, you're going for an evaluation."

Clara wanted to run, but her legs could barely hold her up.

"Can I change clothes?" she asked.

"I'll go with her," the female officer said.

Upstairs, Clara tried to get to the bathroom. "Please, I just need—"

"You can change here," the officer said, standing in the bedroom doorway. "I need to keep you in sight."

"The bathroom, please—there's something—"

"You can use the facilities at the hospital."

Clara changed into jeans and a loose shirt, her hands shaking so badly the officer had to help with the buttons. Every instinct screamed to get to the bathroom, to grab the journal, to show them the lipstick message. But the officer wouldn't let her out of sight.

Back downstairs, Julian had packed a small bag. "Some clothes, her insurance card," he told the officers. "I'll follow in my car."

They walked her to the police cruiser. Not handcuffed, but the female officer's hand stayed on her elbow. Clara looked back at the house. Behind that toilet was everything—her journal, her desperate message. But no one would look for it.

As they drove away, Clara saw Mavis in her yard, Stanley's cage on the porch. She tried to wave, but Mavis was focused on filling Stanley's water dish. The parrot, though—Stanley saw her. He squawked and tilted his head, watching the police car drive away.

Northwood Pines Psychiatric Hospital sat on the outskirts of town. The windows had that subtle reinforcement that said no one leaves without permission.

Dr. Graves waited in the intake area, as if she'd been expecting them.

"Officers," she said smoothly. "I'm Dr. Alana Graves, Clara's psychiatrist. I've been expecting this, unfortunately."

"You have?" the male officer asked.

"She's been deteriorating rapidly. Paranoid delusions, medication non-compliance. I specifically recommended involuntary commitment if she became violent." Dr. Graves pulled out a folder. "I have her records here."

The intake nurse barely looked at Clara, taking her information from Julian and Dr. Graves instead.

"History of anxiety disorder," Dr. Graves was saying. "Recently escalated to paranoid delusions, dissociative episodes. This morning's violent incident is consistent with her pattern."

"I wasn't violent," Clara tried to say, but no one was listening.

They took her belongings, even checking the lining of her clothes and the soles of her shoes. Looking for contraband, sharp objects, anything she might use to hurt herself or others. They found nothing because there was nothing to find.

Ward 7 was exactly what she'd feared. Locked doors with small windows. Cameras in corners.

Her room was small. Bed bolted to the floor. Reinforced window looking out at a parking lot. A camera in the corner, red light blinking.

"Medication time," a nurse announced, entering with a small paper cup.

"What is it?"

"Doctor's orders. For the agitation."

Clara had no choice. The nurse watched her swallow, checked her mouth after.

Twenty minutes later, Julian was allowed a brief visit. He sat in the plastic chair, playing the concerned husband perfectly.

"I just want you to get better," he said, loud enough for the nurse in the doorway to hear.

"Please," Clara whispered. "Don't do this."

"Oh, and don't worry about your little hiding spots," he said quietly. "I'll do a thorough cleaning while you're gone."

"Mr. Thorne," the nurse said. "Visiting time is over."

Julian stood, squeezed Clara's shoulder for show. "I'll be back tomorrow. Try to rest."

She watched through the reinforced window as he walked to his BMW. Even from here, she could see him whistling.

Supper came on a plastic tray—lukewarm chicken, overcooked vegetables, a cup of juice that tasted like medication. Clara forced herself to eat.

As darkness fell, she heard crying through the wall. Then, later, a whisper through the ventilation grate:

"What's your doctor's name?"

"Dr. Graves."

A long pause. "The fancy one? Dark hair, expensive suits?"

"Yes."

"Be careful with that one." The voice dropped even lower. "She only comes for certain patients. The ones whose families have money."

"What do you mean?"

"I've been here six months. Seen a lot of doctors, a lot of patients. But Graves? She only takes special cases. Private pay. And her patients . . ." Another pause. "They never seem to get better. Only worse."

"Have you told anyone?"

"Told them what? That a doctor visits rich patients? That's not a crime." A bitter laugh. "Besides, who listens to the crazy woman in Ward 7?"

"What's your name?"

"Jane. You?"

"Clara."

"Just be careful. And the day nurse, Brenda? She notices things. Doesn't like Graves much. Might be worth talking to."

After the voice went quiet, Clara searched her sparse room. Under the narrow bed, wedged against the wall, she found a golf pencil—stubby, too short to be considered a weapon.

She grabbed a napkin from her tray. In tiny letters, she wrote: *Journal hidden behind toilet tank at home. Lipstick message on baseboard. Tell Nate. Julian killed Margaret. Aug 1 deadline.*

She folded the napkin until it was smaller than a quarter, then tucked it into the elastic of her sock. If she could get it to this Brenda, maybe—

Clara lay on the narrow bed. Her only hope now was that someone—Nate, maybe Mavis—would find what she'd hidden. That someone would think to look behind an ordinary toilet in an ordinary bathroom and find the evidence that could save her.

Two weeks until August first.

Two weeks until Julian got everything.
Unless someone started listening to a parrot.

10

MONDAY, JULY 17

"GOOD MORNING, MRS. THORNE." A nurse stood next to her bed. Her name tag read *Brenda*. "Time for your medication."

Clara struggled to sit up. The bed beneath her felt damp with sweat.

Brenda set a small paper cup on the bedside table. Three pills—white, round, identical.

"What are they?" Clara's voice came out raspy.

"Doctor's orders." Brenda poured water from a plastic pitcher. But instead of leaving immediately like the other nurses, she lingered, checking Clara's vitals.

"Your heart rate's elevated," Brenda said, making notes on her clipboard. "How are you feeling?"

"Foggy. Restless."

Brenda nodded, writing more than seemed necessary for those two words. "These doses are . . ." She paused, glanced toward the door, "Have you been on antipsychotics before?"

"No. Just anxiety medication. Years ago."

Another note. "I see."

Clara wanted to say more, to beg for help, but another nurse appeared in the doorway.

"Brenda? Dr. Graves is here for rounds."

"Of course." Brenda watched Clara swallow the pills, checked her mouth, then left with the other nurse.

Twenty minutes later, Dr. Graves entered without knocking. She wore a black suit with sharp shoulders, a silver caduceus brooch on her lapel—the medical symbol feeling more like a badge of authority than healing. Her dark hair was pulled back in a twist. "How are we feeling this morning, Clara?"

We. As if they were a team.

"The medication makes me sick."

"Adjustment period. Perfectly normal." Dr. Graves didn't look up from her clipboard. "Your husband mentioned you were agitated yesterday. Threatening him with a knife?"

"I was making toast—"

"The mind can construct elaborate justifications for violent impulses." She finally looked at Clara. "I'm adjusting your treatment protocol. Different formulation, should help with the agitation."

"I don't need—"

"What you need, Mrs. Thorne, is to trust the process. Your husband will visit this afternoon. Perhaps seeing him will help ground you in reality." She made another note. "We'll schedule your competency evaluation for Thursday. Three days should give the medication time to stabilize you."

"Competency evaluation?"

"Standard procedure for involuntary holds. Don't worry, if you're improving, it's just a formality.

Of course, if you're not improving, we'll need to discuss more intensive treatments."

She left before Clara could respond.

Breakfast was served in a common area, a beige room with round tables and windows that didn't open. Clara sat alone, pushing scrambled eggs around her plastic plate. The medication made everything taste like cardboard.

"You're the new one."

Clara looked up. A woman sat down across from her—mid-forties, brown hair streaked with gray. "I'm Jane. Room twelve. I heard you talking through the vent last night."

Clara recognized the voice immediately. "You warned me about Dr. Graves."

"Did I?" Jane took a bite of toast. "I say a lot of things. They tell me I'm delusional." She leaned forward slightly. "But I notice things. Been here long enough to see patterns."

"What kind of patterns?"

"The kind that would sound crazy if I said them out loud." Jane glanced around the room. "There was another woman, couple months back. Mrs. Ellington. Pretty thing, younger than you. Her husband was devoted, he visited every day, brought flowers."

"What happened to her?"

"Transferred to a long-term facility upstate. After she signed some papers." Jane shrugged. "Or maybe I imagined it. Hard to tell sometimes, with all the medication."

Clara lifted her juice cup. Was Jane trying to warn her, or was this the rambling of someone who'd been institutionalized too long?

"Why are you here?" Clara asked.

"Rich father. Embarrassing daughter. I was going to tell people something I shouldn't." Jane smiled bitterly. "Funny how mental illness can strike so suddenly when family secrets are involved."

After breakfast was art therapy. Clara sat at a table with paper and crayons, her hands too unsteady to draw anything recognizable. The medications made her feel both exhausted and agitated, like she needed to run but couldn't lift her legs.

Brenda appeared beside her, checking another patient's blood pressure.

"Difficult to focus?" Brenda asked, not looking at Clara directly.

"Everything's difficult."

"Mm." Brenda adjusted the blood pressure cuff on the other patient. "Thursday mornings, a patient advocate visits. Reviews treatment plans, medications. If someone felt their dosage was . . . excessive, they could request a review."

"That's the same day as my evaluation."

"Is it?"

She moved on before Clara could respond.

The morning crawled by. Clara tried to read a magazine in the common room, but the words swam on the page. She dozed in a chair, waking to find drool on her chin. Other patients moved around her like ghosts—some muttering to themselves, others sitting in silent stupor.

After lunch, soup she could barely taste, a nurse announced visiting hours.

Julian arrived looking like he'd stepped from a magazine. Pressed khakis and a blue oxford shirt. He carried a small bag and a bouquet of daisies.

"How are you feeling?" He sat across from her in the visiting room, reaching for her hand.

"You know how I'm feeling. You put me here."

"Clara, you were waving a knife. The police saw you. Multiple witnesses saw your confusion at the farmer's market. This is for your own good."

"I was making toast."

"You were having an episode. But that's why you're here, to get better." He pulled papers from the bag. "I brought some things from home. Your insurance cards, some clothes. And this."

He set a document on the table. *Power of Attorney.*

"It's temporary," he said. "Just while you're recovering. The estate paperwork needs to be filed, bills need to be paid. I can't access anything without your signature."

Clara stared at the document. "No."

"Honey, be reasonable. How can you make financial decisions in your current state?"

"I said no."

"Clara, I'm trying to help you. The estate has to be properly managed. There are deadlines."

"What deadlines?"

"Tax filings, investment transfers. It's all very complicated." He pushed the paper closer. "Just sign it. Let me take care of things while you focus on getting better."

"No."

He sat back, and for the first time, she saw real frustration on his face. Then it was gone, replaced by concern.

"Dr. Graves mentioned you might resist treatment. She's scheduled an evaluation for Thursday. If you're not showing improvement . . ." He let the threat hang. "There are other options. More intensive therapies."

"Like what?"

"Let's not worry about that. Just think about the power of attorney. I need it signed soon."

Clara said nothing.

"Oh," he said, standing to leave. "I cleaned the house thoroughly. Got rid of all those hiding spots you'd created. Fresh start when you come home."

Clara's heart sank. Did he find the journal and lipstick message?

That afternoon, there was a group therapy session led by a Dr. Hoffman, a tired-looking man who seemed to be going through the motions.

"Would anyone like to share?" he asked without enthusiasm.

Clara raised her hand. "My husband . . . he's trying to steal my inheritance."

Several patients looked up. Dr. Hoffman sighed.

"Clara, this has already been discussed with you. Paranoid ideation is common with your condition."

"But it's true—"

"The mind can make anything feel true." He turned to another patient. "Walter? How about you?"

Walter, an elderly man, started talking about the radio. "They're sending messages through it. Even when it's unplugged. I hear them at night."

Another patient, a middle-aged woman, rocked slightly in her chair. "The neighbors are watching me through the walls. I can feel their eyes."

"My food tastes wrong," a younger woman added. "They're putting things in it. Chemicals."

Clara sounded just like them. Her story—Julian drugging her coffee, conspiring with Dr. Graves—fit perfectly alongside their delusions.

"You see?" Dr. Hoffman said, looking at Clara. "The mind creates these narratives to make sense of confusion and fear. It's a symptom, not reality."

Jane sat quietly in the corner, observing everything but saying nothing.

"Let's practice grounding techniques," Dr. Hoffman continued. "Focus on what you can actually see and touch, not what you think might be happening."

Clara wanted to scream that she *had* seen things—the pills, the documents, Julian's lies. But looking around at the other patients, each convinced of their own impossible truths, she felt her certainty wavering. What if she really was just like them?

That evening, after another tasteless meal and more medication, Clara lay in her narrow bed, staring at the ceiling. The napkin with her desperate message was still tucked in her sock, but who could she give it to? Who would believe her?

A soft knock on her door made her sit up. Jane slipped inside, closing the door quietly behind her.

"Can't stay long," Jane whispered. "Night rounds in twenty minutes."

"In group today, I sounded just like them. Like every paranoid patient in here."

"Did you?" Jane sat on the edge of the bed. "Listen, I've been here eight months. I've seen a lot of patients come through. Most are genuinely ill—the radio voices, the wall watchers. But Dr. Graves's private patients? They're different."

"You told me they're inconvenient patients, at least to their families. How are they different?"

"They come in coherent, just confused. Insisting someone's trying to hurt them. Then they deteriorate fast, much faster than normal psychiatric progression. More confused. More medicated." Jane paused. "Mrs. Ellington was like that. Clear one week, barely conscious the next. Then her husband took her home. Or somewhere. No one really knows."

"But that could just be the illness progressing—"

"Could be." Jane said. "Or could be something else. The thing is, in here, you'll never be able to prove which one it is."

"That's what Dr. Grave's is doing to me."

"Maybe. Or maybe we're both crazy." Jane smiled sadly. "That's the thing about this place. After a while, you can't tell the difference."

She stood to leave, then paused. "That nurse, Brenda. She's been here forever. Follows rules, but she notices things. And Thursday, your evaluation day? That patient advocate she mentioned? If you could stay clear-headed enough to talk to her . . ."

"How? The medication—"

"That's the problem, isn't it?" Jane slipped out, leaving Clara alone.

Clara tried to stay awake, to think clearly despite the medication. Thursday was three days away. Her competency evaluation. The patient advocate. It might be her only chance.

But what if she was wrong? What if Julian was right, and grief had broken something in her mind? The other patients' stories could be coincidences, or her drugged brain finding patterns that weren't there.

Just before she fell asleep, she heard something outside her window. A bird calling, loud and insistent. It sounded almost like . . . but no. Stanley was miles away, in his cage on Mavis's porch. Wasn't he?

The sound came again. Then, clear as day, she heard it: a perfect imitation of Julian's whistle. That Sinatra tune he loved.

Clara pressed her face against the window, searching the dark parking lot. Nothing. Just cars and empty space and the distant streetlights.

The medication was playing tricks on her. Had to be.

Tomorrow was Tuesday, July 18th. Thirteen days until August first. But Thursday's evaluation felt like the real deadline. If she failed that, if Dr. Graves convinced them she needed more intensive treatment . . .

Clara clutched the napkin in her sock. Three days to find someone who would listen.

Three days to prove she wasn't crazy.

Or three days to discover that she was.

11

TUESDAY, JULY 18

CLARA WOKE TO FIND Brenda taking her blood pressure.

"How are we feeling today?" Brenda asked.

"Tired. The medication—"

"Yes, about that. Dr. Graves has ordered an increase. Starting today."

"More?"

"Significantly more. Your evaluation is in two days. Dr. Graves wants you stabilized." Brenda set down the medication cup, four pills now instead of three. "I need to document that you've taken these."

Clara picked up the cup, noticed Brenda had turned slightly away, checking her watch.

"Oh, I'm running late. Take those quickly, please."

Clara palmed one pill, swallowed the other three. When Brenda turned back, Clara showed her empty mouth.

"Good." Brenda leaned down to adjust Clara's blanket, her voice dropping to barely a whisper. "Thursday's evaluation. Stay as clear as you can."

After Brenda left, Clara crushed the pill and hid it in the trash can. One less poison in her system, though three were still too many.

Breakfast in the common room was the usual beige affair. Clara sat with Jane, who pushed rubbery eggs around her plate.

"You look better than yesterday," Jane said.

"Nurse Brenda—"

"Careful." Jane glanced to the cameras in the corners. "They record everything."

They ate in silence for a moment before Jane spoke again. "Did you know they have a library cart that comes around Thursdays? Same day as evaluations. The volunteer who runs it is very . . . observant."

Before Clara could ask more, Dr. Hoffman shuffled in for morning group therapy.

"Let's discuss coping strategies," he said.

Clara barely listened. Instead, she thought of Thursday. Two days to prepare for an evaluation that would determine the rest of her life.

After group, Clara was told she had a visitor.

Julian waited in the visiting room. He'd brought another bouquet, roses this time.

"You look tired," he said, reaching for her hand.

Clara pulled back. "The medication—"

"Is helping you get better." He set a folder on the table. "We need to discuss practical matters."

"More power of attorney forms?"

"You need to be realistic, Clara. Your evaluation is Thursday. If you're not showing improvement . . ." He opened the folder. "Long-term facilities aren't pleasant.

But if you cooperate, show that you're trying to get better, things could go differently."

"Cooperate meaning sign over my inheritance."

"Cooperate meaning trust your husband. I'm trying to help you. Do you know what happens to non-compliant patients? The treatments they use?"

"Is that a threat?"

"It's reality." He pushed the papers closer. "Sign these, show the evaluation board you're capable of making rational decisions, and you could be home by next week."

Clara stared at the papers. "No."

"You're making a mistake."

"Mr. Thorne?" A nurse appeared in the doorway. "Visiting time is over."

Julian stood, straightening his shirt. "Think about what I said. Thursday's evaluation will determine everything."

After he left, Clara returned to her room. Twenty minutes later, Jane slipped through her doorway.

"Heard something you should know." Jane sat on the edge of Clara's bed, voice low. "Brenda was talking to another nurse at the medication cart. Didn't know I was in the hallway."

Clara leaned closer.

"Your dose, Graves has you fifty percent above maximum recommended. That's not treatment, that's . . ." Jane paused. "Well, that's something a patient advocate would be very interested to know. If someone happened to mention it during an evaluation."

"How do you know what the maximum—"

"Eight months here, you learn things. You learn what different medications look like, what normal doses are." Jane glanced toward the door. "Brenda said it."

"Thursday's evaluation . . ."

"Right. Andrea Willis is the advocate's name. She's independent, not connected to Graves."

The afternoon brought more medication, a nurse she didn't recognize watched her swallow every pill. She tried to walk to the common room but had to grip the wall to stay upright.

"Steady there." Jane appeared beside her, guiding her to a chair. "The increase?"

Clara nodded, unable to form words.

"They did this to Mrs. Ellington too. Day before her evaluation. She could barely speak when they asked her questions." Jane glanced around, then pressed something into Clara's hand.

"Hide this. For Thursday."

Clara looked down. A small packet of instant coffee.

"Caffeine," Jane whispered. "Helps clear the fog a little. Not much, but maybe enough."

That evening, Dr. Graves made an unexpected appearance.

"Your husband is concerned about your resistance to treatment," she said, standing at the foot of Clara's bed. "It suggests the paranoid ideation is stronger than we thought."

"I'm not paranoid."

"No? You believe your husband murdered your aunt. You think I'm conspiring against you. You've told other patients these delusions. This is textbook paranoid schizophrenia, Mrs. Thorne."

"It's not—"

"Your evaluation is in forty-eight hours. The board will expect to see improvement. Cooperation. Acceptance of your condition. If they don't see those things, I'll recommend longterm intensive treatment. There's a facility that's very remote. Very . . . thorough."

The threat was clear.

After Dr. Graves left, Clara lay in the bed, fighting the medication's pull toward unconsciousness.

Later, through the walls, Clara heard other patients settling for the night. Someone was crying. Someone else was praying.

Tomorrow was Wednesday. One more day of increased medication. Then Thursday, the evaluation that would determine whether she got out or disappeared into some remote facility.

But even if they kept her here, Julian couldn't just sign papers in her name. That would be forgery. He needed her declared legally incompetent and have a guardian appointed by the court. That took time, hearings, evidence. Or he needed her to sign the power of attorney herself. Which meant, they wouldn't just warehouse her somewhere. They'd keep her medicated enough to be compliant but functional enough to hold a pen. Dr. Graves would document that Clara had "moments of clarity" where she "voluntarily" signed documents.

That's why he kept bringing the papers. Eventually, with enough drugs, enough isolation, enough Dr. Graves telling her she was sick, she might actually sign them. And it would be perfectly legal. A mentally ill woman making a "rational decision" to let her loving husband help with finances.

The horror of it was its legitimacy. Everything done with proper forms, medical documentation, witnessed signatures.

Clara closed her eyes, trying to hold onto consciousness, to plan, to think. But the medication was too strong.

Through the fog, one thought remained clear: Thursday. Everything depended on Thursday.

12

WEDNESDAY, JULY 19

JULIAN ADJUSTED HIS ITALIAN silk tie in the elevator's polished steel doors. The law offices of Patterson & Associates occupied the entire thirty-second floor of the Renaissance Tower in Grand Rapids. Patterson specialized in what he called "wealth preservation strategies" for clients who valued discretion above all else.

"Mr. Thorne." Patterson emerged from his corner office. "Melissa said this was urgent."

"Family matter. Delicate situation."

Patterson's office overlooked the Grand River. Floor-to-ceiling windows and leather furniture arranged around a coffee table. No family photos, no personal touches, just the tools of a man who solved problems for people who paid well to keep those problems private.

"Coffee? Scotch?"

"Coffee's fine." Julian settled into the leather chair, crossing his legs. "I need advice about protecting assets. My wife has . . . mental health issues."

Patterson poured from a silver service. "I see. And these issues affect her judgment?"

"Severely. She's currently hospitalized. Involuntary commitment." Julian accepted the cup, noting Patterson's lack of surprise. "The doctors say it could be long-term."

"Ah." Patterson returned to his chair. "And there are substantial assets involved?"

"Two-point-eight million. Recent inheritance." Julian sipped his coffee—excellent, as expected. "I need to ensure proper management while she's . . . incapacitated."

"Several options available." Patterson pulled out a legal pad and gold pen. "The conservative approach would be a conservatorship proceeding. Court-appointed oversight, very legitimate. Takes time, though, six months minimum."

"Time is a factor."

"Creditors?"

Julian paused, swirling his coffee in a slow circle. "Business obligations. August first deadline."

Patterson made a note without looking up. "Then we consider the expedited route. Durable Power of Attorney. Much faster, assuming she signed one."

"She hasn't. Yet."

"Ah." Patterson set down his pen. "You need her to sign while she's hospitalized."

"The doctors say she has moments of clarity. Periods when the medication allows rational thought."

"How convenient." Patterson said. "The key is documentation. Your psychiatrist will need to note these lucid intervals carefully. Medical records showing she understood what she was signing, made rational decisions about her financial affairs."

"Dr. Graves is very thorough."

"She'll need to be. The POA must be executed during one of these documented lucid periods. Not too lucid, we don't want her questioning the necessity. But competent enough that the signature holds legal weight."

Julian leaned forward. "What's the window?"

"Sweet spot is about forty-eight hours after medication adjustment. Still manageable, but coherent enough for legal purposes." Patterson retrieved a file from his desk drawer. "I've handled similar cases. The documentation is crucial."

He opened the file, revealing forms Julian recognized—Power of Attorney templates, but more comprehensive than anything he'd found online.

"Durable POA for finances, separate one for healthcare decisions. This version, unlike most versions,"—Patterson tapped the papers—"is irrevocable once executed. She can't simply change her mind later."

"And if she refuses to sign?"

"Then we pursue conservatorship. Longer process, but more permanent. Court declares her incompetent, appoints you as conservator of the estate. Full legal authority." Patterson shrugged. "Of course, that requires testimony. Medical experts, family members, evidence of incapacity."

"How much evidence?"

"Pattern of irrational behavior. Financial mismanagement. Danger to herself or others. Police reports help. Multiple psychiatric hospitalizations. Documentation of paranoid delusions."

Julian thought of the farmer's market incident, the video on his phone, the knife episode that led to Clara's commitment. All carefully documented.

"Assuming the POA route," Julian said, "what's your fee structure?"

"Twenty percent of assets transferred. Plus hourly consultations. Includes all necessary documentation, coordination with medical staff, legal filings."

"And discretion?"

"Absolute. Attorney-client privilege covers everything we've discussed." Patterson closed the file. "Though I should mention, if your wife's psychiatrist is involved, she'll need similar protection. Medical board investigations can be unpleasant."

Julian smiled, thinking of Alana's expensive tastes, her willingness to bend ethical boundaries for the right price. "Dr. Graves understands the risks."

"Good. Then we proceed with the POA strategy. I'll prepare the documents today. You'll need them ready for the next lucid window."

"How do we ensure the timing?"

"That's between you and the doctor. I don't need those details." Patterson stood, signaling the meeting's end. "But I will say this, the longer she's hospitalized, the stronger your conservatorship case becomes. If the POA doesn't work, we have excellent grounds for the court route."

They shook hands.

"One more thing," Patterson said as Julian reached the door. "These situations sometimes attract outside attention. Family friends, former therapists, people who think they're helping. Make sure your medical documentation covers any interference."

"Already handled."

"Excellent. I'll messenger the documents to your office by end of business."

Julian rode the elevator down, whistling softly. Less than two weeks until August first, and Clara was still fighting. But tomorrow's evaluation gave Alana the perfect opportunity to adjust treatment. A failed evaluation meant stronger medication, and eventually, compliance.

His phone buzzed as he reached the parking garage. Text from Alana: *Patient evaluation tomorrow. She's more resistant than expected.*

Julian typed back: *Adjust medication. Make sure she appears competent yet easily persuaded. Need signing window by Friday.*

Already working on it.

Julian slipped the phone into his jacket, started his BMW. The drive back to Saugatuck would take an hour. Time to review his strategy, ensure every piece was positioned correctly.

Clara was the weak link now—drugged, isolated, facing evaluation that would determine her fate. But she'd proven surprisingly resilient. Even medicated, she fought the narrative he'd constructed. Still claimed she wasn't sick, still refused to sign anything.

That would change. And if she somehow continued to resist, the conservatorship route waited. Either way, the money would be his.

Julian merged onto the highway. He needed to appear composed when he visited Clara this evening. The devoted husband, concerned about her welfare, patiently waiting for her to accept help.

The performance was almost over. Soon, he could stop pretending to care whether Clara lived or died. In fact, once the money was transferred, her continued existence became a liability. Psychiatric patients sometimes had tragic accidents. Suicide was sadly common in long-term facilities.

But that was a problem for another day. Today, the pieces were in motion. Patterson's documents, Alana's medical expertise, his own careful documentation."

Soon Clara Hayes would sign away everything she'd inherited. And Julian Thorne would be two-point-eight million dollars richer.

In Ward 7 of Northwood Pines, Clara lay heavily sedated, unaware that her fate was being decided in marble halls and wood-paneled offices. The only witness to Julian's crimes continued his vigilant watch from a cage on Mavis Potts's porch.

If anyone had been listening carefully enough.

13

WEDNESDAY, JULY 19
CONTINUED

NATE CALLAHAN SAT AT his kitchen table, staring at his phone. Three days since Clara had been taken to Northwood Pines. Three days of blocked calls, refused messages, Julian's voice telling him to stop "harassing" them.

He pressed play on the saved voicemail for the twentieth time.

"Nate?" Clara's voice, slurred and desperate at 3:13 AM Sunday morning. "Nate, please help me. Julian's drugging my coffee. That special blend, it's not coffee, it's—" A crash in the background. "The pills aren't Tylenol. I've been saving them, hiding them. He killed Margaret. I know it sounds crazy but the neighbor's parrot keeps repeating things Julian said about money and August first and—"

Julian's voice in the background: "Clara? Who are you calling?"

"Dr. Graves isn't helping me, she's helping *him*. They're together." The sound of struggle.

"No, give me the phone—"

"She's having an episode." Julian spoke into the phone. "I apologize for the disturbance."

He'd tried calling back immediately. No answer. Called again at 6 AM, 8 AM, 10 AM.

By noon, his number was blocked.

That voicemail was why he believed her. Clara might have anxiety, but she wasn't delusional. The desperation in her voice was real. The specific details—the coffee, the pills, Morrison, August first, even the parrot—were too precise for a psychotic break.

Nate pulled out his notebook, where he'd transcribed every word of the message.

The coffee in his cup had gone cold an hour ago. Spread across the table were notes he'd been making—fragments of conversations with Margaret, Clara's terrified call, the timeline that didn't add up.

Margaret had been right. She'd called him two weeks before her death. "That man is planning something, Nathan. Watch out for Clara when I'm gone. I've already spoken to my lawyer, Gideon Krell. He knows I have concerns. If anything happens, you call him. Don't hesitate."

When I'm gone. Like she knew.

Nate pushed back from the table. Sitting here wasn't helping Clara. He grabbed his keys and headed for the door. Someone in that neighborhood had to know something. And he needed to find out who this Morrison was, and why Clara was so certain he didn't exist.

Mavis Potts was in her front yard, adjusting a tarp over Stanley's cage to provide shade from the afternoon sun. She looked up as Nate approached.

"Oh, Mr. Callahan! How nice to see you. Though I suppose it's not the cheeriest of times, is it?" She pulled off her gardening gloves. "That poor Clara. Taken away by police on Sunday morning. She looked so confused, so frightened."

"You saw it happen?"

"From my kitchen window. Two officers, very official. Julian was so patient with her, even when she was clearly in distress." Mavis shook her head. "Would you like some lemonade? It's so hot today."

"That would be nice, thank you."

As Mavis headed inside, Stanley tilted his head at Nate and squawked. Then, clear as day: "August first. August first."

Nate froze. The parrot ruffled his feathers and continued: "The money's all mine."

"Here we are!" Mavis returned with two glasses. "Oh, is Stanley performing for you? He's been so chatty lately."

Stanley bobbed his head: "Increase the dosage if needed."

"That's very clear," Nate said.

"Oh yes, African Greys are remarkable mimics. He picks up everything." Mavis settled into a wicker chair. "I've actually been recording him for my YouTube channel, 'Stanley Speaks.' Would you like to see?"

She pulled out her phone, swiping to her videos. "This one's from last Saturday."

Nate watched the timestamp: July 15, 2:47 PM. On screen, Stanley performed a medley of sounds—a doorbell, a car alarm, then a man's voice: "She won't remember anything."

"Probably from some TV show," Mavis said. "But the clarity is remarkable, isn't it? I've been documenting everything for the past two weeks. My subscribers love it."

"Could I . . . could I see more of these?"

"Of course! Let me show you the best ones."

For the next twenty minutes, Nate watched Stanley's greatest hits. Each video timestamped:

July 10: "Half a million dollars." July 12: "It has to look like an accident." July 14: "After the funeral, nothing before." July 16: "She won't suspect anything."

"Mrs. Potts," Nate said, "has anyone else heard these recordings?"

"Just my YouTube followers. Only about forty subscribers, I'm afraid. Stanley's not quite viral yet." She laughed. "That elegant doctor asked about them once, though. The one who's been visiting Clara."

"Dr. Graves?"

"Yes! Such a dedicated physician, making house calls. She was very interested in Stanley. Even asked if I could keep him inside more often. Said the noise might disturb Clara's recovery."

Stanley squawked again: "The money's all mine. The money's all mine."

"Could I possibly get copies of these videos? I'm documenting things for Clara. For when she gets better."

"How thoughtful! Of course. What's your email?"

After leaving Mavis's house with twenty-three videos of Stanley's recordings, Nate drove to the public library.

The library's computers were old but functional. Nate started with David Morrison. No financial advisor by that name in Michigan. No LinkedIn profile. No professional licenses. Expanding the search nationwide found twelve David Morrisons in finance, but none matching Julian's description of his "biggest client."

Next, Julian Thorne's professional profile. Registered financial advisor, clean record, client list that didn't include any Morrison. The testimonials were all from retirees, conservative investors. No one who'd panic about portfolios on a Saturday, demanding emergency meetings.

Nate screenshotted everything, emailing it to a new anonymous account he'd just created.

Dr. Alana Graves was more interesting. Her medical license was valid, but digging deeper revealed three malpractice settlements in the past five years. All sealed, but the public court dockets showed a pattern—wealthy patients, sudden psychiatric commitments, disputes over medical decisions.

One name caught his attention: Sarah Ellington versus Dr. Alana Graves and Northwood Pines Psychiatric. Settled out of court two years ago.

Nate printed the pages, then cleared the browser history. From his own phone, he called Krell & Dimond.

"Gideon Krell's office."

"This is Nathan Callahan. I'm a friend of Clara Thorne, formerly Hayes. I have concerns about her aunt Margaret's death and Clara's current situation."

After a pause, he was transferred.

"Mr. Callahan." Krell's said. "How can I help you?"

"Clara's been involuntarily committed. Her husband seems to be trying to access Margaret's estate. I'm concerned—"

"Mr. Callahan, I cannot discuss client matters. However, I can say that Margaret Denham did express certain concerns before her death. She specifically modified her will after several unexpected visits."

"From Julian?"

"I cannot confirm that. But if you have evidence of wrongdoing, I suggest you document it carefully. Legal remedies exist for financial exploitation of vulnerable adults."

"Clara's not vulnerable. She's being drugged."

A long pause. "That's a serious allegation. Do you have proof?"

"I'm working on it."

"Then work quickly. These situations tend to escalate. Good day, Mr. Callahan."

The line went dead.

After leaving the library, Nate sat in his truck, staring at his notes. David Morrison didn't exist, but Julian had to have told Clara something about where these supposed meetings took place.

He pulled out his phone and scrolled through old texts with Clara from weeks ago. There, June 24th:

Clara: Julian's gone to another Morrison emergency. Says he'll be at some office on Wealthy Street for hours.

Nate: On a Saturday?

Clara: Right? But apparently Morrison owns the whole building or something.

Wealthy Street. That narrowed it down. Nate drove slowly along the street, looking for buildings that might house financial offices. Most were clearly retail or restaurants. But one building stood out, a half-vacant office complex with "For Lease" signs in multiple windows.

He parked and approached the security guard in the lobby. "I'm looking for a financial advisor's office. My friend's husband said he meets a client here. David Morrison?"

The guard laughed. "This building's been three-quarters empty for six months. No Morrison here. Never has been in the two years I've worked security."

"You're certain?"

"I know every tenant. Doctor's office on two, law firm on three, rest is vacant. Been that way since Conway Financial went under last winter."

Conway Financial. That rang a bell. Nate pulled out his phone, searched quickly. Conway Financial had been a wealth management firm that collapsed in a fraud scandal. Their offices— this building—had been mostly vacant since.

"What about someone just using the space informally? Meeting clients here even though they don't rent?"

The guard shook his head. "I'd notice. I log every visitor. Nobody's been using these offices for meetings."

Nate thanked him and took photos of the building directory, the vacant offices, the leasing signs with dates.

Back in his truck, he spread his notes across the passenger seat, building a timeline:

Saturday, July 8: Julian claims to meet Morrison, Margaret dies that night

Sunday, July 9: Fake texts from "Margaret," coffee drugging begins

Monday, July 10: Inheritance revealed

Wednesday, July 12: First Dr. Grave's appointment

Sunday, July 16: Police called, Clara committed

The "Morrison meeting" aligned with something suspicious. And Stanley's recordings mentioned August first.

Nate looked at his watch. 3:30 PM. He remembered from years ago, when his grandmother was at a facility, that visiting hours were typically 4-6 PM on weekdays.

He drove back to Clara's neighborhood and parked three houses down, with a clear view of their driveway. At 3:48, Julian's BMW backed out. Nate watched it disappear down the street, then waited another five minutes to be sure.

The spare key was exactly where Clara had shown him last Christmas, under the orchid pot on the front porch. Margaret had given Clara the orchid, he remembered. Said they were survivors, like Clara.

Nate moved quickly but carefully, starting with the kitchen.

The coffee maker sat on the counter, and beside it, that expensive-looking bag Clara had mentioned in her voicemail. "Special blend" written in elegant script, but no brand name, no company logo. Nate photographed the label from every angle, then opened the bag and sniffed. It smelled like coffee.

He pulled a sandwich bag from the drawer and carefully spooned some grounds into it. Evidence for testing. Then he checked the cupboards, no other coffee brands anywhere.

Nate continued searching. Kitchen drawers, bedroom closets, Clara's office. All sanitized. Everything was too clean, too organized. Clara was neat, but not like this. It looked like someone had systematically gone through everything.

But Clara was smart, and she'd learned from years of anxiety to hide things where people wouldn't look. She'd told him once, years ago during a particularly bad episode, that she'd hide important things in "gross places" because she knew her anxiety would make her avoid them, keeping them safe from her own compulsive checking.

The bathroom. He looked behind the toilet. There on the baseboard, hidden where the toilet met the wall. Lipstick writing, small but clear: *July 14 - He's taking me to commit me.*

Nate knelt beside the toilet, and reached behind it. His fingers hit something wedged between the tank and the wall. A journal.

He pulled it out, leather-bound with Clara's initials embossed on the cover. Inside, her handwriting deteriorated page by page. The entries were dated, detailed, and desperate.

Nate photographed everything, then took the journal itself.

In the bedroom trash, he found tissues with white residue. Pills Clara had hidden instead of swallowing. He bagged several.

In Julian's office, Nate sat in front of the password locked computer. Clara had mentioned once that Julian used the same passwords for everything—their anniversary date. The desk lock opened with a simple letter opener.

Inside: credit card statements showing charges at Northwood Pines dated July 5th— before Clara was admitted. Draft power of attorney documents from Patterson & Associates. And a sticky note: *Petrov - $500K by August 1 - FINAL.*

Nate photographed it all, careful to replace everything exactly as he'd found it. He was closing the desk drawer when he heard a car door. He peered through the office blinds. Just Mavis, returning from somewhere. But she was looking toward Clara's house, frowning.

Time to go.

Nate slipped out the back door, locking it behind him. He made it to his truck unseen. He drove two blocks before pulling over, hands shaking with adrenaline.

His phone buzzed, an unknown number. He almost ignored it, but some instinct made him answer.

"Is this Nathan Callahan?" a professional, female voice asked.

"Yes. Who is this?"

"My name is Andrea Willis. I'm an independent patient advocate contracted by the state. I was assigned to review the patient files at Northwood Pines this morning. I came across the file for a Clara Thorne."

Nate sat bolt upright. "Is she okay?"

"She is heavily medicated, but that's not why I'm calling. Your name and number were listed in her chart as an emergency contact, though it appears someone has attempted to strike it out. There were also several notes from her psychiatrist, Dr. Graves, labeling you as a 'destabilizing influence.'"

"Her husband is trying to—"

"Mr. Callahan," Ms. Willis cut in. "I cannot discuss the specifics of a patient's case. My job is to ensure that protocols are followed and patient rights are protected. I am calling you, as a courtesy, to inform you that a competency evaluation for Mrs. Thorne has been scheduled for tomorrow morning at 10 AM. As a person noted in her file, you have a right to be informed of such proceedings."

"Can I be there?"

There was a slight pause. "I don't think so. Attendance is at the discretion of the attending physician and the legal guardian. But now you have the information. What you do with it is up to you. Good day, Mr. Callahan."

The line went dead.

He had it. The journal, the photos, the evidence. Combined with Stanley's recordings and Morrison's non-existence, it might be enough.

But enough for what? Clara's evaluation was tomorrow morning. Adult Protective Services had already told him they couldn't intervene without concrete proof of abuse. The police would defer to the psychiatric professionals.

Nate spent the evening organizing everything into a comprehensive file. The journal entries, carefully scanned. Stanley's videos with timestamps. The Morrison investigation showing the client didn't exist. Photos from Julian's office. The coffee sample he'd bagged for testing. The lipstick message Clara had scrawled behind the toilet.

Tomorrow, after Clara's evaluation, he'd find a lawyer. Tonight, he had more urgent tasks.

He called Adult Protective Services' emergency hotline.

"I need to report financial exploitation and medical abuse of a vulnerable adult," he said when someone answered.

"Is the person in immediate danger?"

"She's been involuntarily committed and is being overmedicated before a competency evaluation tomorrow."

"If she's already in a facility under medical care—"

"The doctor is conspiring with her husband to steal her inheritance."

A pause. "Sir, that's a serious allegation. Do you have proof?"

"I have recordings, journal entries, evidence of drugging—"

"You'll need to file a formal complaint. I can email you the forms."

"She has an evaluation tomorrow morning that could determine—"

"The forms typically take 5-7 business days to process."

Nate hung up in frustration.

Next, he called the medical board's complaint line. After navigating through endless menu options, he reached a voicemail system.

"This is Nathan Callahan," he said after the beep. "I need to report Dr. Alana Graves at Northwood Pines Psychiatric Hospital for conspiring to overmedicate and falsely commit a patient named Clara Thorne for financial gain. I have evidence of prescription fraud, dangerous dosages, and ethical violations. The patient's competency evaluation is tomorrow morning at Northwood Pines. Please, someone investigate before it's too late."

He left his number, knowing no one would hear it until business hours tomorrow.

Finally, he opened his laptop and found email addresses for five attorneys specializing in elder abuse and patient rights. He crafted a detailed message with "URGENT - COMPETENCY EVALUATION TOMORROW 10 AM" in the subject line, attached key pieces of evidence, and sent it to all of them.

Maybe one would respond. Maybe none would. But he'd done everything he could tonight.

Nate stared at Clara's journal, open to an entry from July 11th: *Nate's the only one I trust, but will he believe me? It all sounds so crazy.*

"I believe you."

Tomorrow, he'd find a way to be at that evaluation, even if he had to claim to be Clara's cousin.

He set his alarm for 6 AM and tried to sleep, but Clara's desperate voicemail kept playing in his mind: *"Nate, please help me. Julian's drugging my coffee . . ."*

He'd tried to help after that call—showed up at her door and called repeatedly. But Julian had blocked him at every turn, and the system was designed to believe the husband and the doctor over the concerned friend.

Tomorrow was Thursday, July 20th. Clara's evaluation was at 10 AM. And somehow, some way, he was going to get her out of there.

14

THURSDAY, JULY 20

THE CONFERENCE ROOM REEKED of body odor. Clara sat in a molded plastic chair engineered to be slightly too low, making her feel like a child at a tribunal. A long table stretched before her, where professionals and her husband would decide her future. Her hands were finally steady, courtesy of Jane's instant coffee, she had forced down an hour ago.

Dr. Graves sat at the center of the table, a thick folder spread before her like a queen surveying her map of conquest. To her left, Dr. Hoffman already looked half-asleep. To her right sat Dr. Quin, the independent evaluator, a man who offered Clara a brief nod. Slightly apart from them sat Andrea Willis, the patient advocate, a legal pad and pen her only weapons.

And in the chair designated for family, there was Julian. He wore his concerned husband costume—a shirt deliberately rumpled, as though he'd been too distraught to iron. He leaned forward, elbows on knees, hands tight as if holding himself together on Clara's behalf.

"Good morning, Clara," Dr. Graves said. "How are you feeling today?"

Clara recalled Brenda's advice to keep it simple. "Tired."

"Understandable." Dr. Graves made a note. "Mr. Thorne, would you like to share your observations of Clara's recent behavior?"

Julian cleared his throat, voice quivering with sorrow. "Watching her these past weeks has been . . . unbearable. The lovely woman I married is gone. She used to be vibrant and creative, but now she's often confused and fearful. It's like her past mental issues have returned. I've documented several incidents that might help the panel understand what we're dealing with." He tapped his phone and linked it to the screen on the far wall.

The farmer's market video played first. Clara watched a version of herself she didn't recognize—confused, defensive, her eyes wide with a paranoia that looked utterly convincing on screen. She saw herself denying the brunch with Linda Henderson, a brunch multiple people had apparently witnessed.

"This was last Saturday," Julian said. "Multiple vendors saw her confusion. She had no memory of the day before."

Next came the police bodycam footage. The officer reported: "Subject appeared agitated, pupils dilated, speech slurred. Husband reported she threatened him with a knife."

Clara's throat constricted. "I was making toast."

Dr. Graves didn't look at her. "Clara, please wait until you're addressed."

Julian kept going. Security camera footage from a bank ATM appeared. Clara watched herself, dazed, fumbling with her card, forgetting it entirely as she wandered away. The date flashed: July fourteenth. The day of the brunch she couldn't remember.

Clara gripped the arms of her chair. "I was drugged. Someone slipped something into my drink."

Dr. Hoffman exhaled, and Dr. Quin lifted his pen. "Drugged by whom, Clara?"

"My husband." Her gaze bored into Julian. "He's been putting something in my coffee."

Julian's wounded disbelief was Oscar-worthy. "This is what I mean. She's convinced I'm poisoning her. She's even accused me of murdering her aunt for the inheritance. These delusions, they're becoming more and more elaborate."

"Check on David Morrison," Clara shot back. "Julian was supposed to meet him the night my aunt died. He doesn't exist."

Julian simply opened his wallet and passed a business card to Dr. Quin. "David Morrison, Morrison Investments. I can provide his phone number, his office address. This fixation is part of the lifetime mental illness she has."

"Then call him," Clara challenged. "Call him right now."

"Clara, this isn't productive," Dr. Graves said. "Focusing on these intricate conspiracy theories is a primary symptom of your condition."

Andrea Willis leaned forward. "If the patient makes a specific claim, verifiable or not, it's relevant to our evaluation. If Morrison doesn't exist, that supports your case, Dr. Graves. If he does . . . well."

Dr. Graves's pen paused mid-scratch. "Ms. Willis, we are not here to indulge paranoid fantasies."

Willis didn't back down. "Competency depends on the facts, Dr. Graves."

"I have seventeen documented incidents of paranoid ideation and dissociative episodes," Dr. Graves said, tapping her folder for emphasis. "Including delusions involving myself, her husband, and, if you can believe it, a neighbor's parrot."

The word *parrot* landed like a gavel. A faint smirk passed over Dr. Hoffman's face.

Andrea Willis looked away, her confidence fading.

Clara's desperation spiked. "Stanley isn't just a parrot, he's a mimic. He repeats things. He recorded Julian—"

Dr. Quin's pity was almost unbearable. "Do you realize how that sounds, Clara? That a pet bird is your witness in a conspiracy?"

"I know. I know how it sounds, but it's true. I wrote a message in the bathroom."

Julian's expression was one of profound sadness. "I cleaned the house, Clara. There's nothing there. You were confused about hiding things. The security video showed you throwing out your aunt's journals yourself."

"That wasn't me! I mean, it was, but I was drugged—"

"Mrs. Thorne," Dr. Quin said, "let's change the subject. Tell me about the novel you were writing."

"It's a detective story. Detective Sullivan is investigating a case where the evidence has been manipulated. To make a key witness appear unreliable."

Dr. Quin arched an eyebrow. "An interesting parallel."

"It's not a parallel! I started it months ago, before any of this happened!"

She saw it then, the closed loop. Everything she said, every piece of her life, was now reframed as a symptom. Her creativity was evidence of delusion. Her fear was proof of paranoia.

"I'd like to discuss the medication protocol," Andrea Willis said. "Mrs. Thorne is currently on a cocktail of antipsychotics at dosages that appear to be above the recommended maximum."

Dr. Graves didn't flinch. "The dosages are within the upper therapeutic range, Ms. Willis. Necessary, given the severity and resistance of her condition."

"She appears overmedicated," Willis said. "The psychomotor agitation, the memory gaps; these are known side effects."

"Side effects are an expected part of finding the correct therapeutic balance," Dr. Graves turned to her colleagues for support. "Dr. Hoffman?"

"Absolutely," he mumbled. "Standard procedure. Takes time to calibrate."

Willis sat back. She had made her point, but she was one voice against the medical establishment.

"Clara," Dr. Quin said. "If you were released today, what is the first thing you would do?"

She had to get this right. "I would get a second, independent medical evaluation. And I would stay with my friend, Nate Callahan."

Julian sighed. "The friend who has been attempting to interfere with her treatment. He has been feeding her these paranoid ideas. Clara, you called him at three in the morning, screaming that I was trying to kill you."

Clara's composure cracked. "Because you are!"

Silence.

Dr. Graves closed her folder. Dr. Hoffman shook his head. Even Andrea Willis set down her pen. Clara had just handed them the last piece of evidence they needed.

"We have sufficient information," Graves said. "We recommend a thirty-day hold and more intensive treatment. There is a specialized facility, Pinewood, that is equipped to handle complex cases like this."

"I concur," Dr. Hoffman said.

"Ms. Willis?" Graves prompted.

"For the record, I object," Willis said. "I request a state-appointed independent evaluation."

"Noted," Dr. Graves said. "We will begin the transfer arrangements for Pinewood immediately."

Julian turned to Clara, crocodile tears brimming. "We'll get you the help you need, sweetheart. I promise."

An orderly wheeled Clara back to Ward 7. The caffeine had burned off completely, leaving behind a bone-deep exhaustion. It was over. He had won.

Jane was waiting by her room. "I heard," she whispered as the orderly left. "Pinewood. That's where they send the ones they don't want coming back."

Clara moved to the window. In the parking lot below, a truck was parked near the exit. A figure stood beside it, too far away to see clearly, but she knew that stance. He was looking up at the third floor, at her window. He hadn't given up.

Across town, Nate's phone rang. It was Gideon Krell.

"Mr. Callahan, I just received a call from the patient advocate's office. The evaluation was a disaster, as we feared. They're transferring Clara."

"We have to do something."

"We are. I've been reviewing Margaret's will all morning. She was more clever than any of us knew. She added several codicils, Mr. Callahan. Very specific provisions regarding psychiatric coercion."

"What does that mean?"

"It means, that from beyond the grave, Margaret Denham may have just given us the weapon we need to fight back."

15

FRIDAY, JULY 21

Nate sat across from Gideon Krell's desk, running on a brew of stale coffee and pure adrenaline. He hadn't really slept, not since Krell's call confirming the evaluation had been the disaster he'd feared. He'd arrived at the law office ten minutes before it opened, Clara's journal inside his coaching jacket.

"So they're transferring her to a facility called Pinewood?" Nate said. "It feels like Julian has everything locked down."

Krell steepled his fingers, his expression as gray as the sky outside his window. "The transfer paperwork is likely already in motion. Pinewood is a private, long-term facility. It will be exponentially more difficult to intervene once she is admitted." He paused. "You said you had findings."

Nate pushed Clara's journal across the desk. "She documented everything. The drugging, the gaslighting, the fake client Julian used as an alibi." He followed it with two Ziplock bags; one with the coffee grounds he'd collected, the other with the tissues of pill residue, a photo of the lipstick message from behind the toilet, and the sticky note from Julian's office. "*Petrov. $500K by August 1—FINAL.*"

Krell examined the pathetic collection of evidence. He peered at the photo of the lipstick message. "And you are prepared to testify that you found this . . . where, precisely?"

"Behind the toilet in her master bathroom."

"While you were in the house without the owner's permission."

"I had to get proof," Nate said, shifting in his chair.

Krell's gaze lingered on the final item Nate presented: a printout of Mavis Potts's YouTube channel.

The lawyer removed his glasses and began polishing them with a silk cloth from his breast pocket. "Let me be perfectly clear, Mr. Callahan. You are proposing that the key witness to a conspiracy involving a multimillion-dollar estate is an African Grey parrot with a modest social media following."

"The bird repeats what Julian said," Nate insisted, leaning forward. "He's a living recorder. It's corroboration."

Krell replaced his glasses. "Your investigative methods are, shall we say, *unorthodox*, Mr. Callahan. But they do corroborate Margaret's final concerns."

He unlocked a desk drawer and removed a single key attached to a simple metal tag. "Margaret Denham was a woman who believed in contingencies. When she revised her will, she also established a safety deposit box at First National Bank. The contents were to be accessed by me under the condition of what she termed 'an unnatural silencing of my niece, Clara.'"

Nate stared at the key. "Her commitment to Northwood Pines?"

"Constitutes an unnatural silencing." Krell stood, grabbing a trench coat. "Shall we?"

Krell insisted on driving his own silver Mercedes. Nate's foot slammed down on a phantom brake pedal as Krell pulled into traffic with the calm of a man who believed turn signals were a sign of emotional weakness. A city bus blared its horn, which he promptly ignored.

"Margaret's codicil regarding psychiatric coercion is a masterwork of legal foresight," the lawyer said, executing a lane change that was less a merge and more a hostile takeover of automotive territory. "She effectively created a failsafe against the very scenario we find ourselves in."

"Right." Nate's eyes were fixed on a delivery truck that Krell was rapidly approaching. "Failsafe. Good."

By the time they reached the bank, Nate was no longer sure if the primary threat to his life was a gaslighting sociopath or an estate attorney with the spatial awareness of a stunned badger. Krell parallel parked in a space clearly designed for a motorcycle, leaving the back half of his car jutting into the street like a dare.

"A remarkably efficient trip," Krell said, smoothing his tie as a passing cyclist offered a rather pointed hand gesture.

Nate pried his fingers from the door handle, fairly certain he had just aged five years.

The vault at First National Bank was a relic from another era—a circular steel door thick enough to withstand a bomb. A bank manager verified Krell's identity and legal documents before escorting them into the chamber.

The manager used his key, then Krell's. With a heavy *clunk*, the lock disengaged. A long, narrow metal box slid free.

In a private viewing room with a single light overhead, Krell placed the box on the table. He lifted the lid. The contents were sparse. On top lay a thick, cream-colored envelope with Krell's name written on it. Beneath it sat a single, small notebook, no bigger than his hand. That was all. There were no other journals, no drives.

Krell picked up the letter and, producing a silver letter opener from his briefcase, slid it through the seal. He adjusted his glasses and began to read aloud.

"*Gideon, if you are reading this, it means that snake Julian Thorne has made his move. He has been visiting my home under the pretense of concern for Clara, but his questions are all about assets, about Clara's history with anxiety, about her mother's fragility. He is building a story, brick by brick, to tear my niece down.*"

Nate could picture Julian perfectly, turning on the charm.

"*He is a performer, and a good one. He will make everyone believe Clara is unstable. He will isolate her, medicate her, and convince her that she is the problem. He asked about the strength of the banisters on my staircase, Gideon. Who asks such a thing?*"

A cold dread washed over Nate.

"I have installed new cameras in the greenhouse. The footage saves automatically to a secure cloud server. He doesn't know about it. The login credentials are in the small notebook. Use it all. Protect her. The world is full of men who will call a woman crazy when she is in their way. Do not let this one succeed. He has the morals of a rattlesnake and the charm to match."

The room was silent when Krell finished. He folded the letter and placed it carefully back on the table.

"She knew," Nate said. "She knew exactly what he was."

"Margaret was an excellent judge of character." Krell picked up the small notebook. He opened it to the first page. On it was a URL, a username, and a long, complex password.

Underneath it, a single line:
The truth is in the greenhouse.

16

FRIDAY, JULY 21 CONTINUED

BACK IN KRELL'S OFFICE, the lawyer placed the two Ziploc bags containing the coffee grounds and pill residue into a larger, evidence-style bag and sealed it. Every second wasted felt like a betrayal to Clara, locked away while they sat in this climate-controlled room free of the stench of urine.

"My private investigator, Tom, will have this couriered to a forensic lab in Ann Arbor," Krell said as he wrote out a label. "I'll request an expedited toxicology screen. We should have preliminary results by Monday." He picked up his desk phone, his instructions to Tom a rapid-fire burst of legal and logistical jargon that ended with, "And the chain of custody must be impeccable. I want no room for error. The invoice, as always, will be substantial. Pay it."

While Krell arranged for the collection of physical evidence, he gestured toward his own laptop. "The login credentials, Mr. Callahan, if you please. I left my crystal ball at home."

Krell opened his briefcase and retrieved the notebook they had recovered from the safety deposit box. He placed it on the desk between them, opening it to the first page.

Nate leaned forward, his eyes scanning the spidery script. He read the URL aloud, watching as Krell typed with two methodical, painfully slow fingers.

"Username is 'MDenhamOrchid,'" Nate said. He waited for Krell to finish the entry. "Password is . . ." He read out the long, complex string of letters, numbers, and symbols Margaret had recorded.

Krell entered the last character and hit enter. A loading icon spun in the center of the screen.

"Please work," Nate whispered as he moved next to Krell so that he could see the screen.

The page finally loaded, revealing a single, neatly organized folder labeled: *Greenhouse.* Inside were dozens of video files, each named with a date and time. Krell clicked on the folder for July, the entries a mundane log of an old woman's life until the final file. It was dated Saturday, July 8th. The night Margaret died.

"Here we go," Nate said

Krell double-clicked the file.

The video opened, showing the interior of the greenhouse from a high corner angle. The quality was surprisingly clear. It was late afternoon, sunlight shined through the glass panes, illuminating rows of orchids in bloom. Margaret Denham moved through the frame, tending to her plants. She wore a gardening apron over a floral dress. She looked healthy, nothing like a woman who was hours away from a fatal fall.

They watched in silence for several minutes as Margaret worked, the scene peaceful. Then, a shadow fell across the glass door at the far end of the greenhouse. Nate leaned closer to the screen. The door opened, and Julian Thorne stepped inside. He was wearing the same clothes Nate had seen in Clara's photos from that weekend. He carried no flowers, no gift, just a predatory smile.

On screen, Margaret turned, her body stiffening at the sight of him. She said something, but there was no audio.

Julian responded, his hands spread in a placating gesture that looked utterly false. He walked toward her. He pointed toward the staircase inside the main house, visible through the connecting doorway. Margaret shook her head, taking a step back. He took another step closer, his body language moving from persuasion to intimidation.

Margaret backed away, bumping into a potting table and sending a small terracotta pot tumbling to the floor, where it shattered. Julian reached out, placing a hand on her arm. She tried to pull away, but he held firm, his grip visibly tight. He spoke again, his face close to hers.

Then, Julian looked up, scanning the greenhouse. He froze. His gaze swept the corners of the room, and for a terrifying second, it felt like he was looking directly at them through the screen. He'd spotted the camera.

A slow, chilling smile spread across his face. He said something to Margaret, something that made her flinch, then released her arm and walked directly toward the camera.

The last thing they saw before the screen went black was Julian's handsome face filling the frame, his hand reaching up to cover the lens.

Nate let out a breath. "He disabled it."

"But not before it recorded him there," Krell said. "At the scene. On the night of her death. This contradicts his alibi and establishes clear intent."

Krell's phone rang. "Tom. What do you have?"

Nate listened, watching Krell's face. The lawyer made a series of quick notes on a legal pad.

"Excellent," Krell said. "Send me the full report, encrypted." He ended the call and looked at Nate. "My investigator has been busy. The security guard at the Wealthy Street office building confirms no one by the name of David Morrison has ever been a tenant. His logs for the past six months show no visitor by that name. Furthermore, he has obtained traffic camera footage from the evening of July eighth."

Krell turned the legal pad toward Nate. On it, he'd written: *Julian Thorne, BMW, License Plate J7T-453, photographed 8:14 PM, intersection of Blue Star Highway and 64th Street.*

Nate felt a surge of triumph. "That's less than a mile from Margaret's estate. His whole alibi is a lie."

"Indeed," Krell said. "The fictional Mr. Morrison has been proven to be just that. And Mr. Thorne has been placed at the scene of the crime with clear malice." He tapped the blank screen. "This is the proof we need. It's enough for an emergency injunction."

"To stop the transfer to Pinewood? Is there time?" Nate asked.

"To start. I'll draft the motion immediately. With any luck, we can get a judge to issue a temporary restraining order, freezing Julian's access to the estate and halting any changes to Clara's medical care until we can present the full evidence."

Nate watched him, a sliver of hope finally breaking through. "Do you think it will work?"

Krell paused, his hand on the phone, his gaze meeting Nate's. "Judges are cautious, Mr. Callahan. They dislike emergency motions on a Friday afternoon, and the system is built to protect medical authority. But a conspiracy to commit murder, supported by video evidence and a demonstrably false alibi?" He smiled. "That tends to get their attention."

17

FRIDAY, July 21 CONTINUED

The needle went into the IV port like a whisper of ice. Clara watched Dr. Graves depress the plunger. The clear liquid disappeared into the tubing, and within seconds, a strange warmth spread through her chest.

"This is our new transfer preparation protocol," Dr. Graves said, withdrawing the needle. "Specifically formulated for patients transitioning to long-term facilities. You'll find it quite pleasant, actually."

Pleasant. Her hands, which had been clenched in her lap on the examination chair, relaxed without her permission. The fluorescent lights in the medical room seemed to dim, though she knew they hadn't changed. Everything took on a gauzy quality, like looking through frosted glass.

"How do you feel, Clara?" Dr. Graves's asked.

Clara opened her mouth to say *drugged*, to say *stop*, but what came out was, "Floating."

"Good. That's exactly right." Dr. Graves made a note on her clipboard. "Your husband will be here shortly for his visit. Won't that be nice?"

Nice. Yes, visits were nice. Clara nodded.

The room's edges had gone soft. Clara noticed her reflection in the metal paper towel dispenser. She looked like a doll, glassy and vacant. The thought should have frightened her, but the drug had wrapped her in cotton, muffling even her fear.

"I'll have the nurse come in to check your vitals," Dr. Graves said, moving toward the door. "Your husband should arrive within the hour. Try to stay alert for him."

Alert. Clara almost laughed, but the impulse died somewhere between her brain and her mouth. She couldn't even lift her hand to brush the hair from her face.

Time became elastic. Minutes or hours passed, Clara couldn't tell. The wall clock's second hand swept in lazy circles. A nurse came in, took her blood pressure, said something Clara didn't quite catch. The blood pressure cuff squeezed her arm, a distant pressure like being hugged by a cloud.

Then Julian was there, filling the doorway with his phoney concern. He wore a gray suit today, the one that made his eyes look darker.

"Hello, sweetheart." He pulled a chair close, too close to the exam chair. "Dr. Graves says you're doing better today."

Clara tried to focus on his face, but it kept sliding out of alignment. "Julian."

"That's right." He reached into his briefcase. "I brought some papers we need to discuss. Just routine things, but they need your signature."

Papers. Clara watched him spread them across the small table used to hold medical instruments. The words swam on the page like black fish in white water.

"This is a Power of Attorney," Julian said. "It just means I can help you with financial decisions while you're getting treatment. You want me to help you, don't you?"

Clara knew there was a reason she should say no, but it hovered just beyond her reach. Her mouth opened, and she heard herself say, "Help."

"Exactly. You're doing so well, Clara. I'm proud of you."

He placed a pen in her hand, wrapping her fingers around it. The pen felt heavy. Julian guided her hand to the signature line.

"Right here," he said. "Just sign your name."

Clara watched her hand move across the paper, forming letters that looked approximately like her name. The signature wavered, but it was close enough. Legal enough.

"Perfect." Julian moved the first document aside, revealing another. "This one is for the estate management. Just temporary, until you're feeling better."

Another signature line appeared before her. Clara signed again, the pen moving in slow, dreamlike strokes.

"One more," he said, producing a third document. "Medical power of attorney. So I can make sure you get the best care."

The pen moved again. Clara's signature became more fluid with each repetition, muscle memory taking over where consciousness failed. She was signing her life away, and she could only watch it happen.

A knock on the door interrupted them. A nurse entered, not Brenda, but someone Clara didn't recognize.

"Mr. Thorne, I can notarize those documents now," the nurse said, pulling a stamp and seal from her pocket.

"Thank you." Julian gathered the papers, arranging them neatly. "I appreciate your discretion in this matter."

The nurse took the papers to the desk in the corner. The notary stamp came down with a definitive thunk. Once. Twice. Three times. Each sound felt like a door closing.

"All done," the nurse said, handing the documents back to Julian. "Everything's legal and binding now."

Legal and binding. Julian tucked the papers into his briefcase. He'd won. Whatever game they'd been playing, he'd won, and Clara had helped him do it.

"You did wonderfully." Julian leaned over to kiss her forehead. His lips were cold. "Rest now. The transfer to Pinewood will happen soon, and you'll need your strength."

Pinewood. The name triggered a panic that couldn't quite break through the pharmaceutical calm. Clara tried to speak, to protest, but her tongue felt useless.

Julian stood. "I'll see you tomorrow, sweetheart. Sleep well."

He left, taking with him any chance Clara had of fighting back. She sat on the clinic chair, staring at the space where the papers had been, her hand still curled as if holding the pen.

Through the window, she could see the parking lot, where Julian's BMW sat gleaming in the afternoon sun. She watched him emerge from the building, briefcase in hand, and check his phone.

The transfer preparation drug kept her floating, untethered from her own distress. She knew she should feel something—rage, fear, desperation—but it was like trying to grab smoke.

The nurse checked the IV port in Clara's arm. "The medication will wear off in a few hours," she said. "You might feel confused when it does. That's normal."

Normal. Nothing about this was normal. Clara wanted to say that, but all that came out was a sigh.

"Your transfer is scheduled for tomorrow afternoon. Pinewood is a very nice facility. Very quiet. You'll have plenty of time to rest there."

Rest. Or disappear. Clara understood with perfect clarity: this wasn't treatment. It was burial.

18

FRIDAY, JULY 21 (EVENING)

JULIAN ENTERED THE MARRIOTT bar at 10:09 PM, shaking off the July humidity as he passed through the revolving doors into the climate-controlled lobby.

The bar was on the mezzanine level, half-hidden by frosted glass partitions. Alana had chosen their usual corner table, the one with a view of the river and complete visibility of anyone approaching. She wore a black sheath dress, her dark hair pulled back to reveal her neck.

She didn't look up from her phone when he sat down. "The documents are filed?"

"Signed, notarized, and legally binding." Julian signaled the bartender. "She could barely hold the pen."

"The transfer preparation medication worked perfectly." Alana said. "By tomorrow night, she'll be miles from anyone who could help her."

Their drinks arrived—Angel's Envy, neat, with water backs. Julian raised his glass. "To perfect execution."

"To profitable partnerships." Their glasses met with a crystalline note.

Around them, the bar hummed with Friday night energy—business travelers and local professionals unwinding, unaware they were sitting near two people who'd just orchestrated the complete destruction of a woman's life.

"Patterson's wire instructions are ready," Julian said, keeping his voice low. "Monday morning, I start liquidating. By Wednesday, Petrov has his money."

"And my fee?"

"Twenty percent, as agreed. Plus what you've already received."

Alana traced the rim of her glass with one manicured finger. "Our last public meeting should be memorable."

"Agreed." He let his knee brush against hers under the table. "Your room or mine?"

"I took a suite. Thirty-third floor." She slipped the spare key card across the table, their fingers touching briefly in the exchange. "Give me ten minutes."

She left first. Julian waited, finishing his bourbon, letting anticipation build. They'd been planning this for months—the scheme, the theft, and this moment of victory.

The elevator ride felt endless. When he reached the suite, the door was slightly ajar. He found her standing by the floor-to-ceiling windows, the city lights creating a glittering backdrop. She'd removed her heels, making her seem vulnerable.

"Second thoughts?" he asked, moving behind her.

"Never." She turned in his arms, her perfume subtle. "I don't do regret."

Their kiss was fierce, months of careful pretense finally dropped. She pulled his tie loose while he found the hidden zipper of her dress. The expensive fabric pooled at her feet.

"Tell me about the morning," she said against his neck. "Every detail."

"She couldn't even focus on the papers." His hands traced the curve of her spine. "Just kept signing where I pointed. The perfect combination of conscious and compliant."

"The sweet spot," Alana said, undoing his shirt buttons. "Functional enough to be legal, impaired enough to be controlled."

They moved to the bedroom, leaving a trail of clothing. The suite was all clean lines and neutral tones, as impersonal as their relationship, based on mutual benefit and shared appetite for cruelty.

She pulled him down onto the bed. "Tell me," she whispered against his ear, "about the moment she signed. I want every detail."

"Her hand could barely hold the pen." His lips found the hollow of her throat. "She tried to focus on the papers. She looked so lost."

"Perfect," Alana breathed, arching against him. "Absolutely perfect."

Their connection was intense, each movement precise. There was heat between them, but it was the heat of shared conspiracy rather than genuine passion. They came together like two predators celebrating a successful hunt, taking satisfaction not just in each other but in their conquest.

"We destroyed her," Julian said afterwards, his voice filled with dark satisfaction.

"We freed ourselves. Her fortune will fund a dozen more schemes."

They lay intertwined, planning future conspiracies between kisses. The city lights painted shadows across their skin as they moved together again, slower this time, savoring their triumph.

"You know what the best part is?" Alana said later, her head on his chest. "She actually trusted you. Even at the end, some part of her wanted to believe you loved her."

Julian laughed. "Love is just another tool. Like the medication you prescribe."

"Exactly." She shifted to look at him. "Though I have to admit, watching you play the devoted husband was educational."

"And watching you play the concerned doctor?"

"Oscar-worthy, wasn't it?"

They came together once more as dawn approached, their coupling as methodical as their conspiracy, every touch calculated for maximum effect, every whispered word another step in their dark dance of mutual benefit.

As dawn approached, they dressed in silence. Alana fixed her makeup in the bathroom mirror while Julian counted out bills for the room service tip.

"When will you visit her?" Alana asked, applying lipstick.

"Monday. After the banks open. I want to tell her the money's gone."

"Cruel."

"Necessary. The more hopeless she feels, the more likely she is to sign anything else we need."

They left separately, as they'd arrived. Julian whistled Sinatra in the elevator; "Fly Me to the Moon" had never sounded sweeter.

By the time he reached his car, Alana had already texted: *Phase one complete. Begin phase two Monday.*

He deleted the message and drove home to the empty house, where Clara's absence felt like its own kind of victory.

Julian poured himself a celebratory scotch and stood in Clara's office, looking at her half-finished manuscript still open on her laptop. Detective Sullivan would never solve his case. The conspiracy would win.

Just like in real life.

19

SATURDAY, JULY 22

N<small>ATE PULLED INTO</small> N<small>ORTHWOOD</small> Pines' parking lot at 6:47 AM, two hours before visiting hours. He'd barely slept, spending the night reviewing the evidence. Krell had prepared the emergency injunction that would be filed Monday morning. They knew Clara was being transferred to Pinewood, the patient advocate had confirmed that much, but the exact timing was kept deliberately vague. "Within 72 hours" was all the staff would say.

The security guard at the entrance barely glanced up from his newspaper. "Visiting hours start at nine."

"I'm here about Clara Thorne. Family emergency."

The guard sighed, picked up his phone. "Someone here about the Thorne patient . . . Yeah . . . Okay." He hung up. "Wait here."

A nurse appeared five minutes later. "Mr. Callahan?"

"How do you know my name?"

"Your name's on a list. You're not to be admitted to this facility." She held up a paper. "Mr. Thorne's instructions."

"I need to know if Clara's been transferred yet."

"I can't discuss patient information."

"Just tell me if she's still here."

"Transfers to long-term facilities typically happen during night shift. For patient comfort."

"So she's gone."

"I didn't say that."

Nate was turning his truck around when his phone buzzed. Krell's name appeared on the screen.

"They moved her five hours ago," Krell said. "I just got off the phone with the state board. Julian filed the transfer paperwork."

"Can we stop it?"

"She's already there. Pinewood has admitted her."

"Then we go get her."

"With what authority? Julian has medical power of attorney now. Clara signed the documents yesterday."

Nate slammed his fist against his truck. "There has to be something—"

"There is. The injunction. But no judge will hear it until Monday. In the meantime, I'm sending my investigator to Pinewood. We need to document her condition, the facility, everything. Build the case."

"I'm going up there."

"They won't let you see her. You're not on the approved visitor list."

"I don't care. She needs to know we haven't given up."

"Mr. Callahan—Nate. The best thing you can do right now is help me prepare for Monday. We have one shot at this injunction. If we fail, Clara disappears into that system permanently."

Clara woke to the sound of someone screaming. Not sudden scream of surprise, but the low, hopeless wail of someone who'd been screaming for so long it had become routine.

She tried to sit up and discovered she couldn't. Soft restraints held her wrists to the bed frame. The room was smaller than her space at Northwood—no window, just a bare bulb protected by a wire cage and a vent near the ceiling.

"Good morning, Two-Four-Seven."

A nurse stood in the doorway—middle-aged, solid, with the expression of someone who'd stopped seeing patients as people years ago.

"My name is Clara."

"Your name is whatever we call you." The nurse began removing the restraints. "You're in Pinewood Psychiatric Facility, Unit C. Your husband admitted you. You've been sleeping off the transfer medication."

Clara's mouth felt like cotton. "Water?"

"After medication." The nurse produced a syringe. "Hold still."

"What is that?"

"Your prescribed treatment. Arm out."

Clara had no choice. The needle went in the IV port, the plunger depressed, and within seconds a familiar fog began creeping into her thoughts.

"Where exactly is Pinewood?"

"Remote Michigan." The nurse disposed of the syringe. "Your husband was very specific about wanting you to have a fresh start, away from negative influences."

She surely was miles from Nate, from Mavis, from anyone who might help.

"I want to make a phone call."

"Phone privileges are earned through compliance. Minimum two weeks."

"That's illegal. I have rights—"

"You have the rights your guardian allows. Mr. Thorne was very clear about limiting outside contact during your adjustment period."

The nurse left, and Clara forced herself to stand. The room spun slightly, but she managed to reach the door. Locked, of course. Through the small window, she could see a hallway that looked more like a prison than a hospital.

Twenty minutes later, she heard a series of clicks—doors unlocking electronically down the hall. Her own door swung open.

"You're new."

A patient stood in the doorway—a woman perhaps sixty, thin, with the careful movements of someone who'd learned not to make sudden gestures.

"I'm Dorothy. They put new arrivals next to me because I'm *stable*. You're one of Graves's, aren't you?"

"How did you—"

"There's a pattern. Successful women, sudden mental health crisis, wealthy husbands or families. We've got four of them here in Unit C."

Dorothy led Clara to what she generously called the common room; a space with bolted-down furniture and windows covered with thick mesh. Three other women sat at a table, playing cards.

"This is Sarah, Linda, and Catherine," Dorothy said. "We call ourselves the Graves Society."

Sarah looked up from her cards. "Let me guess. Your husband needed money, you started getting confused, and suddenly you're crazy?"

"Something like that."

"Same story, different details," Linda said. She was younger than the others, maybe forty. "My brother needed control of our family trust. Dr. Graves made it happen."

"How long have you been here?"

"Fourteen months."

Clara felt her knees weaken. "Over a year?"

"The medications make time . . . flexible," Catherine said. She hadn't looked up from her cards. "Some days feel like years. Some months pass in a blink."

"But surely someone's looking for you—"

"Who?" Sarah asked. "Our families put us here. Our friends were told we're getting help. And after a few months of no contact, people stop asking."

Dorothy touched Clara's arm gently. "The key is not to fight too hard. They note everything as resistance. Build up enough incidents, and you're here forever."

"There has to be a way out."

"There is," Linda said. "Sign whatever they want. Give them control of everything. Then maybe, if you're lucky, they'll transfer you to a less restrictive facility."

"Where you'll still be drugged," Sarah added. "Just with prettier walls."

A bell rang. The women stood immediately, forming a line.

"Medication time," Dorothy explained. "Don't resist. It's worse if you resist."

Clara watched the others shuffle forward, accepting pills or injections without protest. When her turn came, she held out her arm, feeling like she was surrendering the last piece of herself.

The nurse administering the injection looked younger than the others. As she swabbed Clara's arm, she whispered, "Someone called the state board about you. They're investigating."

Before Clara could respond, the needle was in, the medication flowing. The nurse moved on, leaving Clara wondering if she'd imagined the words.

The afternoon dissolved into a haze. Lunch—or was it supper?—appeared on plastic trays. Clara forced herself to eat, though the food tasted like cardboard soaked in disinfectant.

As evening medication approached, Dorothy sat beside her.

"Here's what they don't tell you," she said quietly. "The doctor here, Morrison, he's not real. I mean, he exists, but he's never actually here. It's all forged signatures, video consultations with someone who might be an actor. Your husband chose this place specifically."

"Morrison," Clara said, the name clicking. "Julian's fake client was named Morrison."

Dorothy nodded. "Sick joke, right? Sending you to a place run by his imaginary friend."

That night, lying in her bed, Clara listened to the sounds of Pinewood—distant crying, the hum of fluorescent lights that never quite turned off, the occasional scream that cut off abruptly. Far from home.

Through the vent came a different sound of whispered voices. Nurses?

"The Thorne woman?"

"Yeah. Husband wants maximum medication. Keep her stable but impaired."

"How long?"

"Indefinitely. He's paying for the platinum package."

Clara closed her eyes, trying to hold onto consciousness even as the drugs pulled her under. Somewhere, Nate was fighting for her, and maybe Krell was building a case. Maybe even Stanley was still repeating Julian's incriminating words.

But here in Unit C, miles from any help, even tomorrow felt like a lifetime away.

20

MONDAY, JULY 24

EVERY TRAFFIC LIGHT TURNED green as he approached, a good omen for what should be his victory lap. Julian adjusted his tie in the rearview mirror of his BMW, parked outside First National Bank. Inside his leather portfolio lay three sets of notarized Power of Attorney documents, each one a golden key to Clara's inheritance.

He whistled a few bars of "Fly Me to the Moon" as he walked through the bank's glass doors. By noon, he'd have access to nearly three million dollars. By Wednesday, Petrov would have his payment, and Clara would be so medicated she'd never question another signature.

"Mr. Thorne!" The bank manager, Richard Henley, approached with a smile. "Right on time. I have the account information pulled up."

"Excellent." Julian settled into the chair across from Henley's desk. "As I mentioned on the phone, my wife's medical situation requires immediate access to her aunt's estate."

Henley nodded sympathetically. "Mental health issues are so difficult for families. Let me just verify the power of attorney documents." He accepted Julian's portfolio, reviewing each page. "Everything appears to be in order. Notarized Friday, medical documentation from Dr. Graves."

"My wife is receiving the best possible care," Julian said, allowing just the right amount of emotional strain to color his voice. "But these facilities are expensive."

"Of course." Henley turned to his computer. "I'll access Mrs. Denham's primary checking account first. Let me just" His typing stopped. He frowned at the screen.

"Is there a problem?"

"I'm getting an unusual flag. Let me refresh the system." More typing. The frown deepened. "I'm afraid there's a complication, Mr. Thorne."

Julian's stomach tightened. "What kind of complication?"

Henley turned his monitor so Julian could see. In bold red letters across Margaret's account information: **COURT HOLD - NO TRANSACTIONS AUTHORIZED**.

"There appears to be an emergency injunction filed against this estate. All accounts are frozen pending a judicial hearing."

Julian stared at the screen. "That's impossible. I have legal power of attorney."

"I understand your confusion, but a court order supersedes any private documentation." Henley clicked through several screens. "The filing was submitted Friday afternoon by . . . Krell & Dimond, LLP. It specifically names you as a party of interest and freezes all asset transfers."

Krell. That sanctimonious old lawyer had somehow discovered—what? Julian forced his breathing to remain steady. "This is clearly a mistake. My wife's family lawyer is simply being overcautious."

"Perhaps. But until the court resolves the matter, my hands are tied. I'm required by law to honor the injunction."

Julian stood, gathering his portfolio. "When can this be resolved?"

"According to the filing, there's a hearing scheduled for Wednesday morning. The court will determine the validity of the injunction at that time."

Wednesday. A few days before Petrov's deadline. "I'll have my attorney contact the court immediately. This is clearly a misunderstanding."

"I hope so, Mr. Thorne. For your wife's sake."

At Community Savings Bank, Julian's second stop, the result was identical. The pleasant woman behind the desk expressed her regrets, but computer systems didn't lie. All of Margaret Denham's accounts—checking, savings, certificates of deposit—were locked down by court order.

"Perhaps you could speak with the judge directly?" she suggested. "Explain your wife's medical situation?"

"I'll certainly explore that option."

By the time he reached Whitmore Investment Group, Julian's confidence had curdled into something approaching panic. Margaret's investment advisor, Donald Whitmore, greeted him with the wariness of a man who'd spent the morning fielding uncomfortable phone calls.

"Mr. Thorne. I received your message about liquidating Mrs. Denham's portfolio, but I'm afraid we have a situation."

"Let me guess. Court injunction?"

"Received the notification Friday evening. All transactions suspended." Whitmore pulled out a thick file. "I also had a rather interesting call from a private investigator this morning. Someone's been asking questions about your visits here over the past few months."

"What kind of questions?"

"About your inquiries regarding Mrs. Denham's asset allocation. Your questions about beneficiary arrangements. The investigator seemed particularly interested in the timing of your visits relative to your aunt-in-law's death."

"I was simply helping family with financial planning—"

"Of course." Whitmore's tone suggested he believed nothing of the sort. "But combined with the injunction, I'm obligated to cooperate fully with any investigation. The court hearing Wednesday should clarify everything."

Julian left the investment office with his portfolio feeling heavier than lead. Three stops, three failures. Every avenue to Margaret's money had been systematically blocked. Someone—Nate, most likely—had been busy over the weekend.

He sat in his BMW in the parking lot, hands trembling as he dialed Petrov's number. The phone rang once.

"Mr. Thorne. I trust you have good news."

"There's been a legal complication. Temporary, but—"

"Explain."

Julian closed his eyes, feeling sweat gather at his collar. "Clara's family attorney filed an emergency motion. The accounts are frozen until Wednesday. But this is fixable, I just need until Wednesday. The court will rule in my favor. I have all the proper documentation—"

"You have seven days until our agreed deadline, Mr. Thorne. But this complication concerns me. How do I know you can deliver if the courts are interfering?"

"The injunction is temporary. Once I win Wednesday's hearing, I'll have full access to the funds. You'll have your money by August first, as promised."

"For your sake, I hope so. But Mr. Thorne? If this legal interference continues, if you've attracted unwanted attention to our arrangement . . ." The pause was ominous. "Well, your wife's life insurance policy is also worth five hundred thousand dollars. One way or another, I will be paid."

"What does that mean?"

"It means, Mr. Thorne, that your wife's life insurance policy becomes relevant to our arrangement.

Five hundred thousand dollars, I believe? Quite sufficient to cover your debt."

The line went dead. Julian stared at his phone, Petrov's implication crystal clear. If he couldn't access Clara's inheritance by Wednesday, Clara herself would have to die to pay his debt.

Julian started the engine, his mind already shifting strategies. He needed Clara functional enough to testify that she wanted him managing her finances. The heavy sedation at Pinewood would have to be reduced, at least temporarily.

He called Dr. Graves. "We have a problem."

Clara woke, confused for a moment where she was. The fog in her head had lifted slightly, not much, but enough to notice the difference. She sat up slowly, testing her balance.

A man Clara assumed must be Dr. Morrison stood in the doorway. Dorothy had warned her about Pinewood's phantom doctor, but seeing him in person for the first time, Clara was struck by his nervous energy. Behind him, the head supervisor Mrs. Albright clutched a clipboard.

"Good afternoon, Clara. You're looking more alert today."

Clara touched her temple, surprised to find her hands steady. "Did you change my medication?"

"Adjusted it, yes. Your husband has requested that you be more responsive for some upcoming legal proceedings."

Legal proceedings. "What kind of legal proceedings?"

Mrs. Albright stepped forward. "There's been some interference from outside parties. People who don't understand your condition or your needs. Your husband requires your cooperation to resolve the matter."

"What kind of cooperation?"

"Simple statements about your care, your wishes regarding your estate." Dr. Morrison stood next to her bed. "Nothing complicated. Just confirmation that you trust your husband to handle your affairs while you recover."

Clara stared at him. "And if I don't cooperate?"

"Then the people causing these complications will succeed in making your recovery much more difficult. They'll drag you through court proceedings, force you to relive traumatic events, subject you to multiple evaluations by strangers who don't understand your case."

"What people? What complications?"

Mrs. Albright and Dr. Morrison exchanged glances. Finally, Mrs. Albright spoke: "Your friend Mr. Callahan has been making accusations. Wild claims about your husband and Dr. Graves. He's convinced a lawyer to file legal motions."

Nate. Nate was fighting for her. He hadn't given up.

"The good news," Dr. Morrison continued, "is that we can resolve this quickly. A few simple statements from you about your wishes, your trust in your husband's judgment, and these outsiders will have no legal standing."

A nurse entered carrying a video camera. Clara's brief hope curdled.

"We'll record your statements today," Dr. Morrison said. "Practice sessions, to prepare you for any formal proceedings. You'll want to sound coherent and decisive."

"What if I refuse?"

Mrs. Albright's grip tightened on her clipboard. "Then your medication returns to previous levels. And your friends' legal efforts become irrelevant."

Clara understood. Cooperate and stay functional, or resist and disappear back into the medicinal mist. But there was something else, the nervousness in their voices suggested they needed her cooperation more than they were admitting.

"When are these legal proceedings?"

"Wednesday morning," Dr. Morrison said. "A court hearing. The judge will determine whether your husband continues to have authority over your care and finances."

Wednesday. Two days away. Clara forced herself to nod compliantly. "I want what's best for everyone."

"Excellent. We'll start with simple questions." Dr. Morrison nodded to the nurse, who began setting up the camera. "Remember, you're grateful for your husband's support. You trust him completely to make decisions in your best interest."

As the camera's red light began blinking, Clara realized this was her chance. Not to cooperate, but to learn exactly what Julian needed from her, and figure out how to deny him everything.

"I'm ready," she said, meeting the camera's eye.

But in her mind, she was planning. Wednesday morning would be her only chance to speak for herself. She had three days to stay strong enough, stay clear enough, to tell the truth when it mattered most.

Outside her window, storm clouds gathered over the Michigan wilderness. Clara couldn't see them, but she could feel the pressure changing. Something was coming.

And for the first time since arriving at Pinewood, she had hope that it might be rescue.

21

MONDAY, JULY 24 (AFTERNOON)

NATE FOLLOWED KRELL THROUGH the courthouse security checkpoint, the lawyer's briefcase their only cargo. They made their way to Judge Harrison's chambers on the third floor.

"Remember," Krell said quietly as they waited outside the judge's door, "Harrison doesn't suffer fools. He agreed to this meeting because the emergency injunction Friday was compelling, but he expects substantial justification for upgrading it."

The door opened, revealing a bailiff who gestured them inside. Judge Harrison's chambers felt like a fortress of legal authority—floor-to-ceiling bookcases, framed diplomas and commendations, an American flag positioned behind a desk. Harrison himself looked every inch the veteran jurist: mid-fifties, steel-gray hair, and the expression of a man who'd heard every possible excuse in his twenty years on the bench.

"Gentlemen." Harrison gestured to the chairs facing his desk. "You have thirty minutes to convince me why I should strengthen an injunction I was already reluctant to grant."

Krell opened his briefcase. "Your Honor, since Friday's filing, we've obtained evidence that transforms this from a civil matter into a criminal conspiracy involving murder, fraud, and ongoing threats to Mrs. Thorne's life."

Harrison's eyebrows rose slightly. "Strong allegations, Mr. Krell. I hope your evidence matches your rhetoric."

"It does." Krell pulled out a sealed evidence bag containing the coffee grounds and pill residue. "Toxicology results from the forensic lab at University of Michigan."

He handed Harrison the lab report. The judge read silently, his expression growing more serious with each page.

"Hallucinogens and antipsychotics," Harrison said finally. "In coffee grounds allegedly from the defendant's kitchen."

"Mrs. Thorne documented being drugged daily," Nate said. "She saved evidence because she knew no one would believe her otherwise."

"And these pills?"

"Psychiatric medications," Krell replied. "Mrs. Thorne palmed them instead of swallowing, preserving evidence of the deception."

Harrison set the report aside. "Compelling, but not conclusive. Mrs. Thorne's mental state has been questioned. A defense attorney would argue she contaminated the samples herself as part of a delusional episode."

Krell nodded. "Which brings us to our second piece of evidence." He pulled out Tom's investigative report. "David Morrison, the client Mr. Thorne claims to have been meeting the night of Margaret Denham's death, doesn't exist."

"Explain."

"No financial advisor by that name in Michigan. No business licenses, no professional credentials. The office building where Mr. Thorne claimed to meet Morrison has been largely vacant for six months. The security guard logs show no visitor by that name ever."

Harrison flipped through the pages, studying the documented phone calls, business searches, and building records. "So his alibi is fabricated."

"Completely. And traffic cameras place his vehicle within a mile of Mrs. Denham's estate at 8:14 PM the night she died, exactly when he claimed to be in a business meeting across town."

"Now we're getting somewhere." Harrison leaned back in his chair. "What else?"

Nate glanced at Krell, then cleared his throat. "Your Honor, this next piece of evidence is . . . unusual."

"I'm listening."

"Mrs. Thorne's neighbor has an African Grey parrot. The bird has been recording conversations from the defendant's house and repeating them."

"Mr. Callahan, are you seriously asking me to consider a bird as a witness?"

"Not as a witness, Your Honor. As a recording device," Krell said, removing his laptop from the briefcase and pulled up Mavis's YouTube channel. "African Greys are remarkable mimics. This particular bird has been inadvertently documenting the conspiracy."

Krell clicked play on the first video. Stanley's clear voice filled the chambers: "The money's all mine. She won't suspect anything."

Harrison leaned forward. "That voice—"

"Julian Thorne's," Nate confirmed. "Recorded July 15th, during one of his supposed client meetings."

Krell played another clip: "Increase the dosage if needed." Then a woman's voice: "After the funeral, nothing before."

"Dr. Alana Graves," Krell said. "And these timestamps correspond exactly with Mrs. Thorne's medical appointments."

Harrison listened to three more recordings, his skepticism giving way to amazement. "This is extraordinary. But without video confirmation—"

"Which brings us to our final piece of evidence." Krell pecked at the keys slowly, squinting at the screen between keystrokes. "Security footage from Mrs. Denham's greenhouse, saved automatically to cloud storage."

The video opened showing Margaret tending her orchids. Then Julian entered the frame, his face clearly visible as he approached the elderly woman. Harrison watched in silence as Julian intimidated Margaret, searched for cameras, and finally disabled the one he'd found.

"The timestamp shows July 8th, 8:14 PM," Krell said quietly. "The exact moment traffic cameras photographed his car nearby."

Harrison removed his glasses, cleaning them slowly. "Mr. Krell, this is no longer a civil asset dispute. This is a murder case."

"Yes, Your Honor."

Harrison immediately reached for his phone. "Carol? Get me District Attorney Mitchell on the line immediately." He covered the mouthpiece. "Gentlemen, I'm upgrading this to a complete asset freeze pending criminal investigation. I'm also ordering an immediate welfare check on Mrs. Thorne."

"Your Honor," Nate said urgently, "she's at a facility called Pinewood, north of here. They've been drugging her heavily."

"Which explains why she can't simply walk away." Harrison spoke into the phone again. "Jim? Harrison here. I need a criminal warrant prepared immediately . . . Yes, murder in the first degree . . . I'll have the evidence couriered within the hour."

He ended the call and turned back to them. "Wednesday's hearing will proceed, but it may become an arraignment instead of a civil matter. I'll have the sheriff's department coordinate with state police. They'll serve the amended court order on both defendants today."

Harrison stood, gathering the evidence. "Be warned, gentlemen. Mr. Thorne is about to discover his perfect crime has been completely unraveled. Desperate men make dangerous choices."

Julian sat in his BMW outside his house, staring at the sheriff's cruiser parked in his driveway. The deputy leaning against it looked bored, but Julian recognized the manila envelope in his hand. Legal papers. The kind that changed everything.

He parked and walked toward the house.

"Julian Thorne?"

"That's right."

"Deputy Reilly, county sheriff. I have court documents for you." The deputy handed him the envelope. "You're also instructed to contact Dr. Alana Graves immediately. She's receiving similar documentation."

Julian accepted the papers. "Thank you, Deputy."

He waited until the cruiser disappeared down the street before ripping open the envelope. The amended court order was thick, official, and devastating. Complete asset freeze. Criminal investigation. Welfare check ordered for Clara. Notice that he was now a person of interest in a homicide investigation.

Julian stumbled inside, his composure finally cracking. A criminal investigation meant they had something solid, but what? His mind raced through possibilities. The greenhouse camera he'd disabled, had there been others? The coffee, the pills; had Clara somehow preserved evidence?

He called Alana.

"What?" Her voice was angry.

"Alana, we have a problem. A big fucking problem."

"I just got served too. Criminal investigation. What the hell did they find?"

"I don't know, but it's serious. Complete asset freeze, homicide investigation. They're treating this like murder."

"How is that possible? We were careful."

"Not careful enough, apparently. That old woman must have had better security than we thought. What if there were other cameras in the greenhouse?"

"This changes everything. If they have any real evidence—"

"We need to cut our losses. Clara becomes a liability now."

"What do you mean?"

Julian paced his kitchen. "She can't testify Wednesday if she's not alive to testify."

"Julian, that's—"

"That's what? Too obvious? Make it look like suicide. Psychiatric patients are high-risk anyway."

A pause, then Alana said, "I could increase her medication to lethal levels. But it needs to happen tonight."

"Then do it. If I'm going down for Margaret's murder anyway, I'm not leaving Clara alive to testify against me."

"Did you ever get those travel packages from Petrov? The ones you mentioned last month?"

"The forged passports? Yes. Cost me twenty thousand I don't have, but they're in my safe. Margaret and James Wilson. Why?"

"Because after tonight, we'll need them. I'll drive up to Pinewood now. Make it look like an adverse reaction to the transfer medications."

"Pack light. We may need to leave without much notice. Text me when it's done."

Julian ended the call and immediately began throwing clothes into a duffel bag. If Alana failed, he'd have to finish Clara himself. Either way, by tomorrow morning, the only witness to his conspiracy would be silenced forever.

22

MONDAY, JULY 24 (EVENING)

THE SHERIFF'S DEPUTY PULLED into Pinewood
Psychiatric Facility at 6:28 PM, two minutes ahead of
schedule. Deputy Carl Brennan had drawn the short
straw for this welfare check, an hour's drive each way
to confirm some rich lady was still breathing. Judge
Harrison's order had come through at 5:30, marked
urgent, which in Brennan's experience usually meant
somebody's lawyer was being paranoid.

He checked in at the front desk, showed his badge
and the court order. The receptionist, a tired-looking
woman with reading glasses on a chain, barely glanced
up from her romance novel.

"Unit C," she said, buzzing him through. "Take
the elevator to the third floor, follow the yellow line."

The psychiatric ward smelled like all psychiatric
wards. Brennan followed the yellow line to the
nurses' station where a heavyset nurse was distributing
medications into small paper cups.

"Deputy Brennan. I need to check on a patient . .
. Clara Thorne."

The nurse sighed. "Room 327. She's fine. Had her
evening meds an hour ago."

"I need to see her."

Another sigh. The nurse abandoned her medication cups and led him down the hallway. She opened Clara's door with a keycard and pushed it open.

Clara lay on the narrow bed, eyes closed, breathing steady. An IV port was taped to her left arm, though no line was currently attached. She looked pale, thin, but stable.

"Satisfied?" the nurse asked.

Brennan stepped closer, watched Clara's chest rise and fall. "She always this out of it?"

"The medications are strong. Doctor's orders." The nurse was already backing toward the door. "I really need to finish evening rounds."

"Yeah, alright." Brennan took one last look at Clara, then followed the nurse out. At 6:45, he was back in his cruiser, typing his report on the mounted laptop: *Patient secure and receiving appropriate medical care. No signs of distress or immediate danger.*

Dr. Alana Graves watched the sheriff's cruiser pull away from her position in the Pinewood parking lot. She'd been sitting in her Mercedes for twenty minutes, medical bag on the passenger seat, waiting. The welfare check was predictable; judges always covered their asses with official visits. But now that box was checked, and the deputy wouldn't be back.

At 7:05, she grabbed her medical bag and walked to the employee entrance, using her ID badge from her consulting work. The night shift had just started, creating the perfect chaos of nurses exchanging reports, discussing problem patients, distracted by the handover protocol.

She took the back stairs to Unit C, avoiding the main nurses' station. The hallway was temporarily empty; evening medications were being distributed in the common area first, before staff moved to individual rooms.

Her badge unlocked Clara's door. Graves slipped inside, closing the door quietly behind her.

Clara didn't stir. The evening medications had done their work, leaving her in a deep, drugged sleep. Perfect.

Graves set her medical bag on the bedside table and pulled out a preloaded syringe. The cocktail inside was elegant in its lethality, a combination that would gradually shut down Clara's cardiac function over the next two to three hours. By the time she went into distress, Graves would be miles away. The death would look like an adverse reaction to the antipsychotic cocktail, a tragic but not uncommon occurrence in psychiatric facilities.

She lifted Clara's left arm, found the IV port. The beauty of the port was that it left no new injection marks. She inserted the syringe into the port and slowly depressed the plunger, watching the clear liquid disappear into Clara's system.

Clara's eyelids fluttered but didn't open. A soft moan escaped her lips.

"Shh," Graves whispered. "It'll all be over soon."

She capped the empty syringe, returned it to her bag, and checked her watch. 7:29 PM. By 10:30, maybe 11, Clara would be dead. Graves had a plane to catch at midnight.

She slipped back out the way she'd come, down the back stairs, out the employee entrance. No one had seen her enter. No one saw her leave. As she drove away, she allowed herself to smile. Julian would be pleased. The final obstacle to their new life had been eliminated.

Nate Callahan had been driving for forty-five minutes, his truck eating up the miles between Saugatuck and Pinewood. He'd tried to wait, tried to trust the system, but something gnawed at him. The criminal investigation was moving forward, but Clara was still trapped in that place.

He pulled into Pinewood's visitor lot at 7:30 PM. Visiting hours were long over, but he had to try. The main entrance was still open.

"I need to see Clara Thorne," he said.

She didn't look up from her book. "Visiting hours are nine to five."

"This is an emergency."

Now she looked up. "Are you on the approved visitor list?"

"No, but—"

"Then you can't see her. That's policy."

"Her husband is trying to kill her. He's under criminal investigation for murder."

"Sir, if you have concerns, you should contact the police."

"The police already know! But something's wrong. I know it."

As he argued, movement in the parking lot caught his eye through the glass doors. A dark sedan was driving away.

"Please," he turned back to the receptionist. "Just call up to Unit C. Make sure she's okay. Her husband just had her committed after she inherited millions. Please, just check on her."

The receptionist sighed heavily. "Sir, if I call the unit and they confirm she's fine, will you leave?"

"Yes."

She picked up the phone, dialed an extension. "Hey, Fran? Yeah, I have someone here concerned about Clara Thorne in 327 . . . Can you just check on her? . . . Yeah, I know, but he won't leave . . . Thanks."

They waited. Through the phone, he could hear distant voices, footsteps.

The receptionist spoke. "She what? . . . Okay . . . No, I'll handle it."

She hung up and looked at Nate. "She's running a slight fever. The nurse is checking her now."

"A fever?"

"Patients sometimes develop fevers. It's not unusual with certain medications—"

"Someone's done something to her!" Nate's voice rose. "That car that just left, who was that? Her husband and her psychiatrist are trying to kill her for the inheritance!"

The receptionist's hand moved toward the security button under her desk. "Sir, you need to calm down or I'll have to call security."

"Call them! Call everyone! A woman is being murdered up there!"

Security arrived in the form of two bored-looking guards who'd clearly dealt with agitated visitors before. As they tried to escort Nate out, he kept shouting.

"Check the visitor logs! See if Dr. Graves was here! She drives a dark Mercedes! Please, Clara's in danger!"

But he was already being firmly guided toward the exit. As the glass doors closed behind him, Nate stood in the parking lot, chest heaving. Through the windows, he could see the receptionist returning to her novel, the guards walking back to their station.

Nobody believed him.

He pulled out his phone and dialed Krell's number. It went to voicemail.

"It's Nate. I'm at Pinewood. Something's wrong with Clara, she has a fever suddenly. I saw a car leaving, might have been Dr. Graves. I think they're trying to kill her tonight."

He hung up and called 911.

"911, what's your emergency?"

"There's an attempted murder in progress at Pinewood Psychiatric Facility. The victim is Clara Thorne in Unit C, Room 327. The suspects are her husband Julian Thorne and Dr. Alana Graves."

"Sir, are you witnessing this attempted murder right now?"

"No, but—"

"Are you inside the facility?"

"They won't let me in."

A pause. "Sir, making false emergency reports is a crime."

"It's not false! Please, just send someone to check on her. Her husband is under investigation for murder and she's the only witness and now she suddenly has a fever and—"

"Sir, we'll make a note of your concern. If you have evidence of a crime, please contact the police department during regular hours."

The line went dead.

Nate stood in the parking lot, staring up at the illuminated windows. Somewhere up there, behind one of those squares of light, Clara was dying, and nobody would listen.

He walked to his truck but didn't get in. Instead, he sat on the tailgate, eyes fixed on the building. He'd stay here all night if he had to. Watch for ambulances. For anything.

At 8:45, his phone buzzed. Krell.

"Mr. Callahan, I got your message. What's happening?"

"Clara has a fever. The nurse said it's nothing, but I saw a car leaving—"

"Stay there, Mr. Callahan. If something is happening, you're our eyes on the ground."

Nate hung up and resumed his vigil, hoping security wouldn't make him leave.

Inside Unit C, the night nurse finished her rounds at 9 PM. Clara Thorne's fever had risen to 101, but that wasn't unusual with the medication cocktail she was on. The nurse made a note in the chart and moved on.

By 9:30, Clara's breathing had grown shallow, but she was alone in her room, the next check not scheduled until 11.

By 10, her heart rate had become erratic, but the monitors at the nurses' station were showing dozens of patients, and one slightly irregular rhythm wasn't enough to trigger immediate concern.

Nate remained in the parking lot, now pacing beside his truck, checking his phone every few minutes for word from Krell.

The race was running, but nobody knew who was winning.

23

MONDAY, JULY 24 (LATE NIGHT)

AT 10:47 PM, THE heart monitor in Room 327 began its irregular dance. The night nurse at the Unit C station noticed the anomaly on her bank of screens, Clara Thorne's heartbeat had developed a concerning arrhythmia. She made a note to check on the patient during her 11 PM rounds.

By 10:54, the arrhythmia had worsened. Clara's breathing became labored and sweat beaded on her forehead.

At 11:02, Gloria entered Room 327 with her medication cart, flipping on the overhead light. What she saw made her freeze. Clara's skin had taken on a grayish pallor, her lips tinged blue.

"Code blue, Unit C, Room 327," Gloria shouted into her radio. "Code blue, I need the crash team now!"

The psychiatric facility erupted into chaos. The crash team, two nurses and the on-call resident, rushed into the room with the emergency cart. Dr. Marcus Webb, three years out of medical school and pulling his second straight shift.

"Get me a tox screen, full panel. And call the hospital, she needs a cardiac unit."

"Do you know what's happening?" Gloria asked while hanging an IV bottle of lactated ringers.

"No, but she could've been over medicated."

In the parking lot, Nate saw the sudden explosion of lights in the third floor windows. Staff running. Then, at 11:14, an ambulance screaming into the lot, paramedics rushing inside with a gurney.

Nate was already recording on his phone when the paramedics emerged, Clara on the gurney, an EMT performing chest compressions as they loaded her into the ambulance. He ran toward them.

"Is she alive?"

"Sir, get back—"

"Is Clara Thorne alive?"

The EMT glanced at him while maintaining compressions. "Who are you?"

"A friend. Someone poisoned her. Test for everything. Dr. Alana Graves did this."

The ambulance doors slammed shut, sirens wailing as it tore out of the parking lot. Nate stood in the red glow of its taillights, then ran back to his truck to follow.

Fifty miles south, at a private airfield, Julian Thorne loaded the last suitcase into the small Cessna. The pilot, a man who specialized in asking no questions for the right price, was already running through his pre-flight check.

"Where's your companion?" the pilot asked.

Julian checked his phone. A text from Alana: *Done. On my way.*

"She'll be here any minute."

Julian had already destroyed his real phone, now carrying only a burner. In his jacket pocket were two Canadian passports—James and Margaret Wilson.

Headlights swept across the tarmac. Alana's Mercedes pulled up beside the plane. She got out carrying a single bag.

"Any problems?" Julian asked.

"None. She'll be dead within the hour."

"You're certain?"

"The dose I gave her would kill a horse. It's done, Julian."

They climbed into the plane. As they taxed toward the runway, Julian mentally calculated their resources. Forty thousand in cash between them, money he'd been skimming for months, plus what Alana had saved. Not much, but enough to disappear for a while. Once Clara was declared dead and the heat died down, they could fight the asset freeze from abroad, claim the inheritance as her grieving widower.

"Control tower, this is Cessna N9847B requesting clearance for takeoff," the pilot said into his radio.

"N9847B, you're cleared for runway two-seven."

The small plane accelerated down the runway and lifted into the night sky at 11:26 PM. Below them, the lights of Michigan fell away. In two hours, they'd land at a small airport in Ontario. By morning, they'd be on an international flight to Mexico City, then Costa Rica, where extradition was nearly impossible if you paid the right people.

Julian looked at Alana. In the dim cabin light, she looked older. This was no longer about passion or even partnership, just mutual survival. They were bound together now by murder.

"No regrets?" he asked.

"About Clara? None. About trusting you? We'll see."

They were allies only as long as it served them both. Julian wondered, not for the first time, which of them would betray the other first.

At the small community hospital, Clara was wheeled into the cardiac intensive care unit at 11:43 PM. Dr. Samuel Archer, the attending physician, reviewed the initial blood work.

"This is a sophisticated cocktail," he told his team. "Digitalis derivatives, calcium channel blockers, something I can't even identify. This was designed to kill."

"Will she make it?" a nurse asked.

"I don't know. We're trying everything, but whoever did this knew exactly what they were doing."

In the waiting room, Nates phone buzzed.

"Any word?" Krell asked.

"Nothing. They won't tell me anything because I'm not family."

"I'm calling Judge Harrison again. We need a warrant for Julian's arrest immediately."

"It might be too late. They could be anywhere by now."

"They're likely running. And Clara might die while they escape."

The clock on the waiting room wall clicked past midnight. It was now Tuesday, July 25th, and Clara Thorne was still alive.

Barely.

24

TUESDAY, JULY 25

THE CLOCK ON THE waiting room wall ticked, each second landing like a drop of water torture. Nate still sat in a hard plastic chair at the small community hospital. A television mounted in the corner displayed an annoying late-night infomercial, but Clara was alive. He clung to that one fact.

He allowed guilt to gnaw at him. Margaret's voice from weeks ago. *Watch out for Clara when I'm gone.* He had listened, but he hadn't understood. He'd let his own damn pragmatism, his need for concrete proof, blind him to a truth that had been staring him in the face, wrapped in a charismatic smile and expensive cashmere.

His phone vibrated, a jarring buzz. He fumbled for it, his hands clumsy. The screen read *GIDEON KRELL*.

"Anything?" Nate pushed himself to his feet and began to pace the small room, the worn linoleum sticky under his sneakers.

"I've done something I haven't done in twenty years of practice," Krell said. "I've woken a federal judge at his home on a Monday night. He was, as you can imagine, profoundly displeased."

Nate stopped pacing. "But did you tell him?"

"I told him his emergency injunction had become the prelude to an attempted murder. I told him our client was in critical condition and that toxicology confirmed she'd been poisoned. I may have used the word 'assassination.' I find judges respond to precise language."

Nate could hear the faint rustle of paper on the other end. "He asked for specifics. Then he asked me to hold. When he came back on the line, he said he was issuing the warrants for Julian Thorne and Alana Graves. Attempted murder, conspiracy, and a raft of financial crimes. He's notifying the FBI and putting out an international alert."

A wave of relief so intense it buckled Nate's knees. He sank back into the chair. "So they'll get them. They'll stop them."

"Nate. This is a victory, but a delayed one. They have a significant head start. They knew the clock was ticking."

Before Nate could respond, a sudden, piercing alarm blared from the hallway, followed by a voice over the intercom: *"Code Blue, ICU. Code Blue, ICU."*

Nate dropped the phone, Krell's voice a distant squawk from the floor. He was out of the chair and in the hallway in a second. A crash cart clattered past him, pushed by a running nurse. Another doctor and nurse sprinted from the opposite direction. They all converged on the double doors of the Intensive Care Unit, Clara's unit.

Nate reached the doors just as they swung shut, catching a glimpse of the chaos inside. He saw her room, saw the flurry of activity. He shoved at the door. "Clara!"

A harried-looking doctor in rumpled green scrubs, intercepted him, holding up a hand. "Sir, you can't go in there."

"That's Clara Thorne! Is she—what's happening?"

"She went into cardiac distress. Her heart is failing. We've stabilized her, but just barely. The toxins . . . this facility isn't equipped to handle this level of toxicology or cardiac care." He looked over Nate's shoulder, toward the main entrance. "A helicopter is on its way from Ann Arbor. We're airlifting her to the University of Michigan Hospital.

Nate turned and spotted his phone on the floor where he'd dropped it, scooped it up without breaking stride, and turned. He burst through the automatic doors of the emergency entrance into the night air, his keys already in his hand. The helicopter might be faster, but he'd be damned if he wasn't on the road to Ann Arbor before it even lifted off the ground.

Clara surfaced slowly, as if from the bottom of a deep, dark lake. The first sound she heard was a steady, rhythmic beep. It was slow, but it was there. The syrupy fog that had been her world for so long was gone, leaving behind a painful clarity. Her body ached between scratchy sheets. There was a tube in her nose, an IV line taped to her wrist, and a strange, metallic taste in her mouth.

She was weak, but her mind . . . her mind was her own. She could think in straight lines again. The thoughts were terrifying, but they were hers.

A man in scrubs stood beside her bed, his back to her as he made a note on a chart. He turned around. He wasn't Dr. Hoffman. He wasn't Julian.

"Welcome back, Mrs. Thorne," he said. "I'm Dr. Pawson. You're at the University of Michigan Hospital. You were airlifted here several hours ago."

Airlifted. The word confirmed a fragmented memory of wind and noise, the sensation of rising. "Why?"

"The toxicology reports came back from the first hospital," Dr. Pawson said. "What was done to you was not medical treatment. You were systematically poisoned with a combination of drugs designed to induce cardiac arrest. Digitalis, beta-blockers, and a chemical agent we're still working to identify. There is no ambiguity here. This was an attempt on your life."

Clara stared at the acoustic tile ceiling. It was one thing to know it, while the world called you delusional. It was another thing entirely to hear it spoken as a clinical fact. The validation was a comfort. But the space it left was immediately filled with devastating grief. The man she had married, the man she had promised her life to, had tried to murder her. The life she thought she had was a lie. A story more twisted than any she had ever written.

"We have you on a protocol to counteract the toxins," the doctor continued, "but your system is under immense strain. You're safe here. We have a sheriff's deputy stationed outside your door."

Safe. The word felt like a language she was just now relearning. She tilted her head, and it was true. Through the glass of the door, she could see a uniformed officer.

"My friend. Nate Callahan. Is he . . .?"

Dr. Pawson smiled. "He's in the waiting room. He hasn't left. He's been demanding updates from anyone in scrubs who gets too close. From what I understand, Mr. Callahan is the reason you're alive."

The tears came then. Julian hadn't won. She was still here. And for the first time in a very long time, Clara Thorne knew, with absolute certainty, that she was not crazy.

25

WEDNESDAY, JULY 26

THE HOSPITAL ROOM WAS boring. The walls, the floor, the bland institutional furniture, all of it was designed to be forgettable, calming. But for Clara, it was the most beautiful room she had ever seen. A uniformed deputy stood just outside the door. For the first time in weeks, she felt the simple, profound luxury of safety.

Nate sat in the visitor's chair in Clara's room. He looked exhausted, his face shadowed with sleeplessness, but his eyes, when they met hers, were clear. He had brought her a cup of tea from the hospital cafeteria, and she held it in her hands, the warmth seeping into her skin.

The door opened, and a man in a suit entered. He was in his mid-forties, with graying temples. He carried a leather-bound legal pad.

"Mrs. Thorne," he said. "I'm District Attorney Jim Mitchell. I'm here to take your statement. Only if you feel up to it, of course."

Clara looked at Nate, who gave her a small, encouraging nod. She took a breath. "I'm ready."

Mitchell pulled a chair to her bedside. "I want you to know, before we begin, that we have the warrants. We have the toxicology reports. We have the evidence your friend Mr. Callahan secured. We believe you. This is not a competency hearing. This is a criminal investigation, and you are the victim and our primary witness. Just tell me what happened. Start wherever you like."

We believe you. The words were a key turning a lock deep inside her. The story she had held in, the one that had festered in the dark while Julian's narrative took over the world, began to spill out. She started with the small things, the insidious seeds of doubt.

"It started with his keys," she said. "He said I'd put them in my purse, but I never touched them. It was such a small thing. I thought I was just . . . scattered."

She recounted the bitter coffee, the "new blend" for stress. She described the blackouts, waking up with no memory of the night before, of a supper she'd apparently eaten, of a chapter of her novel she'd supposedly read to him. As she spoke, the memories, once twisted and weaponized against her, began to straighten out, to find their proper shape.

Mitchell listened, his pen scratching methodically across the page. He didn't interrupt, save for a few clarifying questions. "And this was the same day you received the text messages from your aunt?"

"Yes. He changed the date. I don't know how. He made me think I was losing my mind, that grief was making me delusional."

She told him about the farmer's market, the public performance of her confusion, Julian's concerned-husband act. She described the knife incident, how she'd only been making toast, and how he had twisted her simple action into a threat, a psychotic break for the benefit of the 911 dispatcher.

The hardest part was articulating the gaslighting itself. "He used my history of anxiety against me," she said, the tears she had held back finally beginning to fall. "Every fear I had, he confirmed. Every doubt I had about myself, he magnified. He knew Dr. Kaminski had warned me about catastrophic thinking, so he created a catastrophe and then told me I was just imagining it. He made my own mind my enemy."

Nate reached out and placed his hand over hers.

"He had help," she finished. "Dr. Graves. She was in on it. She prescribed the drugs. She signed the commitment papers. They were going to put me away in Pinewood forever."

Mitchell closed his legal pad. He looked at her, his expression one of grim empathy. "Mrs. Thorne, thank you. You've been incredibly brave. We have everything we need to build a very strong case.

"And regarding the name 'Petrov' on the baseboard, we've already apprehended a Viktor Petrov on unrelated money laundering charges. He's cooperating and has confirmed the details of the debt. You are not in any danger from him."

He stood. "I'm assigning a victim's advocate to you, and the deputy will remain outside your door around the clock. You did nothing wrong. You are not crazy. You are a survivor."

"Have you found them?" she asked. "Julian and Dr. Graves?"

"We have active warrants for their arrest. Their names, faces, and known aliases have been distributed to every law enforcement agency in the country, as well as border patrol. They have nowhere to hide for long."

The yellow crime scene tape stretched across the front door of the charming lakeside house, a garish slash against the perfect blue of the hydrangeas. The place looked the same, but the air around it felt different, tainted. Nate stood on the driveway, watching the forensics team move in and out.

"Mr. Callahan." A detective extended his hand. "Detective Miller. We appreciate you walking us through this."

"Anything to help."

They entered the house. The air inside carried the faint scent of Julian's cologne. Nate's gaze went immediately to the kitchen, to the spot on the countertop where the bread knife had lain.

"So, you found the writing behind the toilet in this bathroom?" Miller asked, gesturing toward the master suite.

"Yes," Nate said, leading the way. "She told me once she hides things in places that make her uncomfortable, so she won't be tempted to check on them."

A forensics technician with a camera was already on his hands and knees. Under the bright glare of his flash, the lipstick message glowed red against the white baseboard: *July 14 - He's taking me to commit me.*

"Got it," the tech said. "Clear as day."

They moved through the house, Nate pointing out the key locations from Clara's journal. In the kitchen, he indicated the half-empty bag of coffee with its elegant, unbranded script and the bottle of "supplements" still on the counter.

"He claimed they were for gut health," Nate explained. "Clara saved some of the pills she pretended to swallow. They're in an evidence bag at Krell's office."

Detective Miller nodded, directing another officer to bag the coffee and the bottle. "We'll get them to the lab. See if they match the toxicology from the hospital."

They moved to Julian's office. Like the rest of the house, it was impeccably clean, almost sterile. The desk was clear except for a laptop and a leather blotter. The books on the shelves were perfectly aligned.

"It's too clean," Miller said, running a gloved finger over a bookshelf. "People who are panicked don't tidy up this well. People who are running, maybe." He scanned the room, his eyes lingering on a framed photograph of a sailboat on the wall behind the desk. It was a generic, impersonal piece of art, the kind one buys to fill a space. It was also hanging just a fraction of an inch crooked.

Miller walked over and straightened the frame. Then he lifted it off the wall. Behind it, flush with the drywall, was the gray metal door of a small wall safe.

"Well, now," the detective said. "That's more like it."

It took a locksmith from the Sheriff's department twenty minutes to drill the lock. Finally, with a heavy *clunk*, the door swung open.

There was no cash. No passports. Instead, the safe contained a single, black leather medical-style bag, the kind a doctor might have carried fifty years ago. Miller carefully lifted it out and placed it on Julian's desk, unzipping it.

The contents were organized. There were boxes of sterile syringes. Vials of clear liquid with pharmaceutical labels. And three prescription bottles.

Miller picked up the first one, holding it under the light. He read the label aloud. "Haloperidol. Patient: Clara Thorne. Prescribing physician: Dr. Alana Graves." He picked up the second. "Lorazepam. Same patient, same doctor." He looked at Nate. "Did Mrs. Thorne know she was being prescribed powerful antipsychotics and sedatives?"

"No," he said. "He told her they were supplements. For gut health."

The detective's gaze returned to the final item in the bag. It was a small, insulated pouch. He unzipped it and carefully pulled out a vial. The label was different. It wasn't a prescription. It was a chemical compound name no one recognized.

"This isn't a prescription," Miller said, holding it up. "This is a raw chemical. The kind you order from a specialty lab." He pulled out his phone, took a photo of the label, and sent it to his forensics lead. "Get this to the state tox lab. Tell them it's a priority. I want to know if it matches the unidentified agent in our victim's bloodwork."

He looked around the office, at the pristine desk, the tasteful art, and then back at the poisoner's kit laid out in the center of it all.

"This wasn't just about making her seem confused," Miller said. "This was a long-term plan. He had a pharmacy in here." He looked at Nate again. "He wasn't just trying to commit her. He was building a case, documenting a mental decline he was creating himself. Every tool he needed to destroy her was right here in this box."

26

THURSDAY, JULY 27

DETECTIVE MILLER FELT THE oppressive atmosphere of Pinewood Psychiatric Facility. He followed the nervous-looking director down Unit C's hallway of locked, identical doors. The place was a warehouse for inconvenient people.

They stopped outside the common room. Inside, a handful of women in gray sweatsuits sat. Miller's presence, along with the two uniformed state troopers flanking him, had sent a ripple of anxious energy through the unit.

"Sarah and Dorothy are in here," the director said, his voice a little too loud. "As I said, their previous charts, signed by Dr. Graves, indicate significant delusional ideation."

"I'm not here to review previous charts, Director," Miller said. "I'm here as the lead detective on a homicide investigation. I have a warrant to conduct interviews." He looked past the director at the women. "And I'm here to listen."

He entered the room, pulling a chair up to a table where two women sat.

"My name is Detective Miller," he began, keeping his voice low. "I know you've been through a terrible ordeal. I also know you've been conditioned not to trust anyone. But I'm here to tell you that Dr. Alana Graves has been charged with attempted murder. You are safe now. And anything you tell me will be taken seriously."

Sarah stared at him. Dorothy wrung her hands in her lap.

"We spoke to a Mrs. Ellington's family this morning," Miller continued softly. "A former patient here. Her husband passed away six months ago. The family has been trying to get access to her, but the trust, managed by her brother, has been stonewalling them. Sound familiar?"

Sarah let out a bitter laugh. "Familiar is the word for it." She leaned forward, her eyes darting to the troopers by the door. "You want to know about Dr. Graves? She was a vulture in designer shoes. She didn't treat patients; she managed assets."

The story, once Sarah started, came out in a torrent. She described the pattern: the arrival of a wealthy, successful woman, often in the midst of a family dispute or inheritance. The initial confusion. The rapid increase in medication. The visits from a concerned husband or brother, always with legal papers in hand.

"She called it finding their 'therapeutic window'," Sarah said with scorn. "That sweet spot where you're just lucid enough to sign a Power of Attorney but too foggy to read the fine print. She did it to us. She did it to Catherine." She gestured to the other women at the table, who were now listening.

Dorothy spoke next, her voice trembling. "The Graves Society, we called ourselves. I think Graves was a serial predator. She'd find a woman's weakness—grief, anxiety, a family secret—and she'd turn it into a cage."

Miller made his notes. Dr. Graves wasn't just an accomplice, she was part of a criminal enterprise, a systematic plundering of lives disguised as psychiatric care. Alana Graves wasn't the tool; she was the architect of a dozen other conspiracies, and Julian Thorne had simply been her latest, most ambitious client.

Detective Miller stared at the computer screen in the forensics lab, a cup of cold coffee forgotten at his elbow. The digital ghost of Julian Thorne was far uglier than the man himself.

"Okay, I'm in," said Zoe, the forensics tech. She had spent the better part of a day peeling back the layers of encryption on Julian's laptop. "First up, the financials he tried to scrub."

On the screen, a spreadsheet appeared, followed by a series of emails. It was all there in black and white: the initial $500,000 loan from a shell corporation controlled by Viktor Petrov. The escalating interest. The threatening emails. The final, non-negotiable deadline.

"August first," Miller read aloud. "He was going to lose everything. Petrov wasn't just a creditor; he was a motive. Julian's desperation had peaked just as Clara's inheritance came through."

"That's not the interesting part," Zoe said. She navigated to a different directory, one hidden inside a nested folder of innocuous tax documents. It was a single, heavily encrypted file labeled simply *'Contingency.'* "This took some work. It's a multi-layered encryption. He really didn't want anyone seeing this."

She typed a final command, and the file opened. It wasn't financial data. It was a dossier. A single, meticulously compiled research document on one person: Dr. Alana Graves.

Miller leaned closer, his eyes scanning the text. It was a predator's playbook on his partner. Julian had documented everything: copies of Alana's three sealed malpractice settlements; detailed notes on her psychological profile, highlighting her pathological narcissism and intellectual arrogance; a full breakdown of her own financial vulnerabilities, including a gambling habit and a portfolio of high-risk investments. He had even noted her preference for a specific, expensive brand of bourbon.

"My God," Miller said. "He was studying her."

"He was planning for her," Zoe corrected, scrolling down. "Look at this." Near the bottom of the file was a section titled *'Leverage Points.'* It was a bulleted list of strategies to discredit her, to report her to the medical board, to expose her to her other wealthy clients. A road map for her complete destruction.

Miller leaned back, the pieces clicking into place. Julian and Alana weren't partners in crime. They were two predators circling the same kill, and Julian, ever the narcissist, had always been planning to be the last one standing. He was never just using Alana as a tool to get to Clara's money. He was using Clara's money as the bait to eventually destroy Alana and take her share, too.

"He wasn't just going to cut her loose," Miller said. "He was going to burn her to the ground."

27

FRIDAY, JULY 28

THE RENTED VILLA WAS a masterpiece of minimalist luxury, all white walls, infinity pool, and floor-to-ceiling glass overlooking the Costa Rican jungle. It was an anonymous paradise, the kind of place that existed outside of reality. Julian, now James Wilson, stood on the terrace, a cup of local coffee in hand, watching a troop of howler monkeys move through the distant canopy. He was a ghost, and this was his ghost's life.

Alana, now Margaret Wilson, emerged from the bedroom, a white silk robe draped over her shoulders. She moved to the bar and poured two glasses of scotch over ice.

"To a successful transition," she said, handing him a glass.

"To us. To the architects of the perfect crime."

He set his drink down. Alana held his gaze for a long moment, a silent acknowledgment passing between them, then turned. The silk robe whispered against her skin as she walked back toward the glass doors leading to the terrace.

She slid the door open, and the humid air of the jungle rushed in with the scent of night-blooming jasmine. She let the robe fall from her shoulders, to the floor's stone tiles, and slipped into the infinity pool. She swam to the edge, resting her arms on the precipice, the water seeming to spill directly into the black-green canopy below.

Julian watched her from the doorway, the very picture of a predator admiring his mate. He shed his own clothes with a deliberate slowness, then followed her into the water, the cool shock of it a baptism into their new life. He came up to her, his body pressing against hers, the water creating a frictionless glide.

"I have to admit," Alana said, her head tilting back, "watching you dismantle her, piece by piece . . . it was masterful."

"And you, my dear doctor," he said, his lips finding the sensitive skin around her ear, "were the perfect instrument of destruction." His hands weren't caressing; they were possessing, sliding from her waist up her ribs.

She rubbed her slick body against his. Their kiss was a collision of appetites. Her fingers dug into his shoulders, her nails scraping lightly as she pulled him closer. His hands tangled in her wet hair, tilting her head back to give him better access to her mouth, her throat. Water sluiced down his chest as he lifted her slightly, her legs wrapping around his waist.

He pushed her back against the wall of the pool, the solid surface a contrast to the weightless suspension of their bodies in the water. The jungle watched, its unseen creatures the only soundtrack to their movements. This was the raw, animalistic thrill of a successful hunt, a shuddering confirmation of their absolute victory.

Afterwards, they floated in the darkness, their shared appetite was sated. The moon cast a silver sheen on the water's surface. Julian felt utterly untouchable, a king in his stolen castle.

Alana swam to the edge and pulled herself from the pool. "Well," she said, reaching for a towel, "let's see if we've made the news."

They moved to the bedroom, a kind of arrogant curiosity on their faces, as a global news network cycled through its headlines. And then, they saw it. Their own faces, clear as day, stared back at them from the screen. The photos were from their professional websites. Below them, a banner in red letters: *FUGITIVES WANTED. JULIAN THORNE & DR. ALANA GRAVES. WANTED FOR CONSPIRACY AND ATTEMPTED MURDER. CONSIDERED ARMED AND DANGEROUS.*

Julian let out a low laugh. "Armed and dangerous. They do love their drama."

Alana simply smirked. "They're looking for Julian Thorne and Alana Graves. Those people don't exist anymore." She gestured around the room. "James and Margaret Wilson, however, are enjoying their retirement."

They were ghosts, untouchable.

Julian laughed again. "Poor Gideon Krell. All that frantic paperwork, freezing domestic accounts that were already being emptied."

Alana raised an eyebrow. "So the wire transfer went through before the freeze?"

"Like a ghost through a wall," Julian said. "He was locking the barn door after the prize stallion was already in another country. The wire I initiated the moment she signed those papers would have cleared long before Krell even got a judge on the phone." He reached for his laptop on the bedside table. "That first transfer is our cushion. The rest of the estate is just a matter of time and paperwork from here."

He sat up, placing the laptop on his legs. He navigated to the encrypted website for the offshore bank in the Cayman Islands, the secondary account he'd set up weeks ago, a financial firewall he was certain Krell could never touch. He typed in the long, complex password.

The page loaded. He clicked on the account summary.

His smile froze.

"What is it?"

Julian stared at the screen, at the two words displayed in bold text: **ACCOUNT FROZEN.** Below it, in smaller print: *By order of an international court, pending criminal investigation.*

"That's impossible," he whispered.

He frantically tried another portal, a different access point. The result was the same. Krell. That sanctimonious, plodding old fool had somehow anticipated him, had reached across borders with a speed Julian hadn't thought possible.

"Julian?" Alana's voice was ice. She leaned over, her eyes scanning the screen.

"He found it," Julian said. "He found everything."

The financial cushion was gone. The victory lap was over. They were no longer wealthy fugitives playing a game. They were just fugitives. Trapped in paradise with nothing but the clothes on their backs and the rapidly dwindling cash in their bags.

The automatic doors of the hospital slid open with a soft whoosh. For Clara, the sensation was overwhelming. The air, thick with the scent of rain-soaked asphalt and car exhaust, felt impossibly rich after weeks of recycled air. The sounds—the distant wail of a siren, the chatter of passing students, the rumble of a city bus—were a chaotic symphony that made her flinch.

She gripped the arms of the wheelchair. Every shadow seemed to stretch and twist, every stranger's face a potential threat. It was the lingering echo of paranoia, the ghost of the illness Julian had manufactured for her. But this time, she knew what it was. It was trauma, not delusion.

Nate's hand came to rest on her shoulder, a warm, steady pressure. "You okay?"

She nodded. Nate was her anchor. He had handled the discharge paperwork, had deflected the well-meaning but pitying glances from the nurses, had stood as a quiet, solid barrier between her and a world she was not yet ready to face.

He pushed the wheelchair along the concrete path toward his truck. The journey felt a hundred miles long. When they reached the passenger side, he helped her to her feet. She was unsteady, her muscles weak from disuse, and she leaned against him for a moment, her face buried in the worn flannel of his shirt.

"I've got you," he said.

Once she was settled in the truck, he shut the door and walked around to the driver's side. For a few moments, they just sat in silence.

Nate put the truck in gear. "The rehab facility is supposed to be nice. Quiet. More like a retreat than a hospital."

Clara looked out the window at the blur of the city passing by. Another institution. Another set of walls, no matter how pleasant. Another place where she would be a patient. She had been a patient long enough.

"No," she said.

Nate glanced at her. "No?"

This was her first real decision as a free woman. The first choice that wasn't about survival, but about living.

"Don't take me there," she said. "Take me to Margaret's."

He didn't argue. He didn't ask why. He simply nodded, and at the next intersection, he made a left turn, heading away from the city and toward the quiet country roads of Allegan County.

As they drove, the urban sprawl gave way to fields and forests. They passed the turnoff for her old house, the one she had shared with Julian. She didn't look back. She was looking forward.

Finally, they turned onto the long, gravel driveway of the Denham Estate. The old Victorian house stood proud and steadfast. It wasn't a prison. It wasn't a hospital. It was an inheritance. It was a legacy.

Nate pulled the truck to a stop and cut the engine. He looked at her. "Are you sure about this, Clara?"

She looked at the house, at the windows that held a lifetime of memories.

"I'm sure," she said, reaching for the door handle. "I'm home."

28

SEPTEMBER (SIX WEEKS LATER)

FOR SIX WEEKS, CLARA had been living in Margaret's house, and for six weeks, she had avoided the greenhouse. It had been the epicenter of the crime that had shattered her world. But today, something had shifted.

She stood in the doorway with a cup of tea. Her body was stronger. The relentless physical therapy had worked the tremors from her muscles, and the healthy food Nate insisted on cooking had brought a healthy color back to her cheeks. She had aired out the rooms, filled the vases with late-season dahlias, and started sleeping through the night without the aid of medication. She was reclaiming the space, one square foot at a time.

On the potting bench, next to an orchid, sat her laptop. Nate had given her the login credentials for the cloud server a month ago, a simple slip of paper he'd left on the kitchen table without a word. She hadn't been ready then. She was ready now.

She typed in the password. The folder labeled *Greenhouse* appeared on the screen. She clicked on the last video file, dated July 8th. She forced herself to press play.

There was Margaret, tending to her beloved orchids. She looked vibrant, a woman with years left to live. Clara felt a pang of grief, but it was different now. This was the grief of loss, not the terror of insanity.

Then, the shadow fell across the door. Julian entered. Clara watched him, not as a wife, but as a detective studying a suspect. The false smile. The body language that shifted from persuasion to intimidation. The way Margaret flinched when he put his hand on her arm. There was no audio, which made it all the more chilling, a silent, destructive ballet.

And then came the moment. The moment Julian's eyes scanned the room and found the camera. His face, for a terrifying second, seemed to look directly at her through the screen. The mask didn't just slip; it evaporated. The concerned husband was gone, replaced by something cold, reptilian. A chilling smile spread across his face before he moved toward the lens, his hand rising to blot out the truth.

Clara closed the laptop. She didn't cry. The tears were for the victim, and she was done being a victim. Resolve settled deep in her bones. She was not just watching a crime; she was bearing witness. She was honoring her aunt's brave act of defiance. Margaret had fought back, and now, it was Clara's turn to see that fight through to the end.

Later that evening, the scent of roasting chicken filled the kitchen. Nate was at the stove, humming along to the radio. As Clara was setting the table, a frantic knock came at the back door.

She opened it to find Mavis Potts, her colorful cardigan slightly askew and a look of exasperation on her face. In her hands, she held a large, covered travel cage.

"Clara, dear, thank heavens you're home," she said, her voice a rushed whisper as if she were a spy on a secret mission. "We have a situation. A domestic crisis."

From under the cover came a disgruntled squawk, followed by a perfectly mimicked, high-pitched voice shrieking, *"Herbert, you put that down this instant!"*

Clara's eyebrows shot up. "Herbert?"

"No, that's me," Mavis sighed, rolling her eyes. "Stanley's taken to imitating my late husband's favorite phrases of mine. It's like being haunted by a very judgmental ghost with feathers." She pushed the cage into Clara's arms. "You have to take him."

"Take him?" Clara laughed, steadying the surprisingly heavy cage. "Mavis, what's going on?"

"It's Penelope," Mavis said. "I thought, you know, with Stanley being a key witness and all the excitement dying down, he might be lonely. So I went to the rescue shelter. I adopted another African Grey. A lovely little thing, but my dear, she is a *floozy*. She won't stop whistling at the mailman, and she's taught Stanley a string of words I'm fairly certain she learned from a sailor. They do not get along. It's all squawking and territorial disputes. My cottage is a war zone."

Just then, Nate appeared at the kitchen door, wiping his hands on a dish towel. "Everything okay out here?"

"Nate, dear, perfect timing," Mavis said, her face brightening. "I was just telling Clara, Stanley here has been moping. Plucking his feathers, refusing his sunflower seeds. The vet says he's fine, but I think he misses the action. He needs a bigger stage. And frankly, Penelope needs the spotlight to herself."

Stanley chose that moment to chime in with perfect clarity, in Mavis's own flustered tone: "*Oh, for heaven's sake, where did I put my glasses?*"

Clara couldn't help it; she burst out laughing. "Mavis, are you giving me Stanley?"

"Of course, dear. A strategic relocation," she said. "Besides, I worry about you in this big house all by yourself. A house needs a little noise. He'll keep the ghosts away."

"Well, you can't leave without eating," Nate said, his lips twitching with amusement. "We have more than enough. Please, Mavis, come in for supper."

Mavis's face softened, her frantic energy melting away into a lonely smile. "Oh. Well, that would be lovely."

They found a perfect spot for Stanley's cage on the screened-in porch, where he could watch the sunset and listen to the crickets. The moment they set him down and took the cover off, the parrot fluffed his feathers, hopped onto his perch, and let out a contented little whistle. He looked around his new domain, then at Clara, and seemed to nod.

Over a supper of roast chicken and potatoes, Mavis held court, telling them stories about Penelope's scandalous vocabulary and her own brief, disastrous foray into online dating. The conversation was light and easy, filling the old house with a warmth it hadn't known in a long time.

Later, as Mavis was getting ready to leave, she paused at the door. "You know," she said, looking at Clara. "He's a good boy, that Nate. The way he looks at you . . . Herbert used to look at me like that. Before I started yelling at him about glasses all the time."

After she left, Clara and Nate stood on the porch. Stanley clicked his beak softly in his cage.

"Did you hear from Gideon Krell today?" Clara asked.

"I did. He filed the initial divorce petition."

"How does that even work? How do you divorce a ghost?"

"It's a process. Krell said it's called a divorce by publication. Since Julian is an international fugitive and can't be served in person, he has to post a public notice in the newspaper for a set number of weeks. If he doesn't respond—and he won't—the judge can grant the divorce in his absence. It's a sure thing. It just takes time."

Time. It was the one thing she had now. The legal knot that still tied her to Julian was frustrating, another piece of his lingering poison, but it wasn't a chain. It was just a thread, and eventually, it would break.

The sun had set, leaving the sky a deep purple. Nate reached out, his hand covering hers where it rested on the railing. His touch was warm. It felt less like the end of a tragedy and more like the beginning of everything else.

29

FEBRUARY (FIVE MONTHS LATER)

THE FEBRUARY SUN STREAMED through the large bay window of Margaret's study. The room, once a formal space, was now Clara's. She had painted the walls a warm cream, replaced the heavy velvet curtains with light linen, and filled the shelves with worn paperbacks and research books on criminal psychology. It was a space of creation.

She sat at a simple oak desk, typing on her laptop. Outside, the bare branches of the old maple tree were etched against a pale blue sky. A fresh layer of snow blanketed the ground. From the other room, she could hear the squawk of Stanley, who was furious that the bird feeder was empty.

Clara looked at the screen, at the final paragraph she had just written. Her protagonist, Detective Sullivan, stood on a windswept pier, having finally exposed the gaslighting conspiracy that had nearly destroyed his key witness. He wasn't triumphant. He was just tired, and quiet, and whole.

She typed the final two words.
The End.

She leaned back in her chair. It wasn't just the end of a novel, it was the end of a narrative that had been forced upon her. For months, Julian had tried to write her story, to cast her as the crazy wife. He had almost succeeded. But now, she had taken the pen back. She had written her own ending. The book wasn't an act of revenge; it was an act of reclamation. She had taken the ugliest, most painful pieces of her life and forged them into a story of resilience.

A car crunched up the gravel driveway, followed by another. Clara looked out the window. A small group of women were walking up the shoveled path to the front door. The first meeting.

She had used a portion of Margaret's inheritance—*her* inheritance—to establish the "Margaret's Voice Foundation." It was a small, local organization for now, a support group and resource center for victims of the kind of insidious, invisible abuse she had endured. The kind that leaves no bruises, only scars on the soul. She thought of the women walking up the path, and even of Mrs. Lee, who she had learned from police reports had been blackmailed by Julian over her son's legal troubles.

She stood and walked out of the study to greet them. She wasn't a victim anymore. She wasn't a patient. She was the woman who was going to let them in.

The humidity in the small room was a physical presence, making the peeling paint on the walls sweat and the single, bare bulb in the ceiling seem to swim in a hazy halo. The air, thick with the scent of stale beer, salt, and decay, was too heavy to breathe properly. Julian, or what was left of him, stared at the cracked plaster, listening to the relentless rhythm of the waves crashing on the seedy beach just a few yards away.

Their paradise had become a prison cell with a better view. The last of the cash had run out three weeks ago, forcing them from their sleek, anonymous villa to this one-room hovel in a town that catered to backpackers and fugitives.

Alana sat on the edge of the lumpy mattress, methodically cleaning her fingernails with the tip of a cheap knife. Her expensive clothes were gone, sold for a fraction of their worth. Her composure was frayed, leaving behind a simmering resentment.

"There's a fishing boat leaving for Panama at dawn," she said, not looking at him. "The captain will take passengers. For a price."

"With what money, Alana? The money you lost on that pathetic online poker game?"

She finally looked up. "Don't you dare. The money *you* failed to secure. The brilliant, foolproof plan of the master manipulator. How did that work out for you, Julian? That plodding old lawyer and the high school football coach . . . they broke you in less than a month."

"They got lucky." He pushed himself off the rickety chair. "If you had been more careful, if you hadn't drawn attention to yourself with your house calls—"

"Drew attention?" She stood, the knife still in her hand. "I was the one doing the real work, taking the real risks, while you were playing the part of the grieving husband! You were so blinded by your own reflection you couldn't see that the world didn't revolve around you. You underestimated all of them. The wife. The friend. The old woman with the parrot."

She laughed an ugly sound that held no humor. "A parrot, Julian. You were brought down by a goddamn parrot. Do you have any idea how pathetic that is?"

He lunged then, his rage finally boiling over. He grabbed her wrist, twisting it until the knife clattered to the floor. "I was the architect of this! It was my plan!"

"It was a failure!" she screamed, her face inches from his, her voice raw with a fury that matched his own. "And you are a failure! A cheap, dime-store sociopath who couldn't even outsmart a bird."

Their partnership, forged in cold ambition, had finally dissolved, leaving only the toxic sludge of their mutual contempt. They were no longer allies. They were just two desperate animals trapped in a cage, and there was only one way out.

30

JULY (FIVE MONTHS LATER)

THE MUGGY BEACH BAR air smelled of frying fish. Ashley, a paralegal from Chicago on a much-needed solo vacation, nursed a warm Imperial, scrolling through her phone. She was a true-crime junkie, her podcast queue a catalog of missing people and cold cases. This trip was supposed to be an escape from all that, but paradise, it turned out, could be a little boring.

A loud, ugly argument erupted from a nearby table. The voices were American.

"—my fault?" a man's voice snarled. "I wasn't the one with a history of malpractice settlements a high school kid could find on Google! Do we really have to keep rehashing this!"

"Oh, please," a woman's voice shot back. "You were so busy admiring your own reflection you let a football coach and a parrot dismantle your 'perfect' plan. A parrot, Julian! Do you have any idea how pathetic you are?"

Ashley froze, her thumb hovering over a picture of a sloth. *Julian.* The name snagged on something in her memory. She risked a glance. The couple were haggard, their faces thin and burnt by the sun, a world away from the polished, professional photos she'd seen on the airport TV a week ago. But it was them. The dreary, handsome man. The desperate, elegant woman. The infamous "Parrot Witness" killers.

Ashley grew excited. This wasn't a podcast. This was real.

Her training, the hundreds of hours spent listening to detectives and profilers, kicked in. *Don't stare. Act normal. Get evidence.* She pretended to text a friend. She swiped to the camera and hit record, angling the lens toward the arguing couple.

"If you had just kept your head down," Julian seethed, "we'd be fine. But you had to get greedy. You couldn't resist playing God."

"And you couldn't resist playing the victim," Alana mocked. "Poor Julian, betrayed by his crazy wife. The inheritance was right there, and you let it slip through your fingers because you were too arrogant to see what was right in front of you!"

Ashley had to get this to someone. She opened a text to her best friend back in Chicago. *OMG CALL FBI. SERIOUSLY. I FOUND THE PARROT WITNESS KILLERS. LIVE. SENDING LOCATION PIN. GO NOW.*

She hit send, then stood up. "*El baño?*" she asked the bartender. He grunted and pointed toward a beaded curtain. She slipped behind it and dialed the local emergency number, praying she could remember the Spanish for *international fugitives.*

The evening light in Margaret's—no, *their*—house was soft and golden. A year had passed. A lifetime. Clara sat curled on the sofa, her feet tucked under her, a laptop balanced on her knees. Beside her, Nate was scrolling through a website, an amused smile on his face.

"Okay, I'm just saying," he said, pointing at the screen, "a taco truck is a perfectly legitimate catering option for a wedding."

Clara laughed, a sound that was easy now. "We are not having a taco truck at our wedding, Nate Callahan. Margaret would haunt us for a century."

"Your aunt would have loved it. She appreciated things that were modest and brilliant. Like you." He leaned over and kissed her.

They were engaged. The ring, a simple sapphire that had been Margaret's. The divorce from Julian had been finalized three months ago, a quiet, anticlimactic proceeding in a courtroom he'd never entered. A ghost, legally exorcised.

On the local news, a segment began. *"And a year ago today,"* the anchor said, *"the quiet lakeside communities were rocked by the 'Parrot Witness' case . . ."*

Julian's handsome, smiling face filled the screen, followed by Alana's cool, professional one. Nate reached for her hand, his fingers lacing through hers. The fugitives, the anchor continued, were still at large, believed to be somewhere in Central America.

Clara looked at Nate. Julian and Alana hadn't escaped. They were just trapped in a different kind of prison, one they had built for themselves. She was the one who was free.

As Julian looked up from his drink, he was struck with horror as a sound suddenly filled the air. It wasn't a siren. It wasn't a shout. It was a ringtone, chirping from the tourist's phone. A tinny, perfectly clear, and utterly absurd recording. A sound that had traveled a thousand miles and a full year to deliver the final verdict.

It was Stanley's voice.

"The money's all mine!"

The End

Don't Close the Book Just Yet ...

Enjoyed the story?
If you liked [Book Title], the best way to support the author is by leaving a short review.
Review it on your [favorite store] — even just a few words can help others discover the book.
Thank you for reading!

* * *

Want to read more?
Sign up for Connie Myres' newsletter and get updates, free stories, and exclusive sneak peeks:
https://www.ConnieMyres.com
Follow Connie on:
X/Twitter https://twitter.com/ConnieMyres
YouTube https://youtube.com/@ConnieMyres

ALSO BY CONNIE MYRES

CONNIE MYRES

Suspense Stories #1: Raven's Ridge, Lucifer's Island, Sinister Attachments
WATCH FOR SPOOKY SHORTS
Spooky Shorts A-G: A Collection of Creepy Short Stories
Apple Pie, Black-Eyed Kids, Creature, Dungeon, Electric, Fairy, Genie, House, Ice, Joker, Kiss, Lucid, Minion, Neighbor (Upcoming: Obelisk, Pattern, Quest, Rumor, Squatch, Time, Underworld, Visitor, Wolf, X-axis, Yellow, ZoZo)
The complete list of books can be found at:
ConnieMyres.com
or
My universal book link:
https://books2read.com/conniemyres/

About the Author

CONNIE S. MYRES is a novelist who writes psychological thrillers that explore the darker side of love and trust. She also writes horror, mystery, and science fiction. When not crafting stories about ordinary people in extraordinary danger, she works on her new hobby, junk journaling. She lives in Michigan, with her family and way too many projects to complete.

Connie's website is ConnieMyres.com.

FEATHER AND FERMION PUBLISHING

Feather and Fermion Publishing is a Michigan-based publisher that was founded in 2014. Our mission is to provide readers with thrilling and entertaining stories across a variety of genres, including horror, mystery, suspense, thriller, science fiction, and fantasy. We publish original fiction under our two imprints: Oort Cloud Books and White-Knuckle Books.

Author Connie Myres owns Feather and Fermion Publishing.

www.ingramcontent.com/pod-product-compliance
Lightning Source LLC
Chambersburg PA
CBHW022134240626
47153CB00007B/2355